Palmer Park

WILLIAM ERIC GRAHAM

To order additional copies of this book, contact:
Xlibris Corporation
1-888-795-4274
www.Xlibris.com
Orders@Xlibris.com
17562

Dedication

To Mom and Dad for showing me how to succeed at whatever I put my mind to and always being there. I love you both deeply.

ACKNOWLEDGMENTS

The first thing I need to do is something I don't do enough: thank God. I thank God for blessing me with life and good health. I want to thank my wife and best friend, Pam, also my boys, Shane and Eric. You guys are my life. The love we share as a family is the most important thing to me. I'll always be here for you. I have to thank my parents, Horatio and Ruby Graham. I love both of you more than words can say. I'm blessed to have you both in my life. My sisters, Lynda Logan, Dr. Bernadine Martin, my brother, Horatio III, and all my nieces and nephews, I love you guys very much. Much love also (too many names to mention, you know who you are) to my extended family in Mt. Clemens, St. Clair Shores, and Chesterfield Township.

Thanks to Dr. Bernadine Denning and Mr. Blaine Denning, Blaine, Roz, and their boys. Thanks for summers at the lake and the after-school jobs at the milk and wine companies. Much love. Love also to Big Ernie and Ann, to my cousins, Ernie, Terry, Kim, and Tony, you all keep the party goin'! (Thanks for those Lions tickets, Ernie).

To my friends on the East Coast (DeDe&Tracy) and West (Stephanie and her crew, Tony T.), what's up!

Thanks to the Utica Trim Learning Lab. A big shout out to the Utica crew, the old "line one" crew, and the brothers from the 7-mile "Y." WHAT'S UP!

A special thanks to the members of I.D. (Kevin, Bill, Bud, Rick C, and Carol). We put some serious music out there. Much thanks to my right-hand man, Darrell Parks, for the excellent cover and author photos (and those parties!). Also thanks to the eastside crew for providing inspiration. (What's up, Turbo, Brent&Nancy, Sylvia, and Joe Jude)

Finally, big thanks to John Ridley, Walter Wager, Stephen King, and Donald Goines.

Nathan Littlejohn was a street hustler. Frank Collazo was a businessman. From their different worlds, a force driven from the illegal operations of the local mob would bring them together.

Two murders from over twenty-five years ago would force them to be allies, something the two men wouldn't have thought possible.

In the next twenty-four hours, the lives of ten people would be changed forever as violence erupted with swift and sudden fury.

The mob boss who ruled Detroit with an iron fist would make sure of it.

And it all happens within one square mile of the Motor City called Palmer Park.

CHAPTER ONE

The man in 4C looked at the clock on the wall of his small apartment. 2 A.M. Instead of winding down after a long day's work, having a beer and relaxing with Sportscenter, he was wired up and pacing the floor. He kept looking out the window every few minutes, wondering if the next siren he heard was for him. That's what participating in armed robbery will do to your nerves. It takes a while to come down from the rush. Eight hours ago, he was an urban commando, a soldier who didn't represent any government agency, fighting the battles that living in the streets of the city required. The battles he fought didn't involve overthrowing crooked governments, saving people from insane rulers, or bringing freedom to lands that so desperately needed it. No, the war this man participates in is a drug war: the type of war that is played out every day in every major U.S. city. It's ignored by the nightly news. But if you live here, you were drafted every day, seven days a week, twenty-four hours a day. The truth is, it didn't matter which side you were on. You were in until you left the hood, one way or another. That's what the battle for crack does to neighborhoods. It destroys them from the inside out, making it impossible for life to go on undisturbed. But if you're careful, smart, and a little lucky, you can survive. That's how the man in 4C saw the situation. It was all about survival, and he was ready to thrive.

"Man, I would love to see the look on Johnny's face when he finds out he's been hit. News is gonna travel fast in this city."

Hank Littlejohn made a mark on the city tonight. Along with his younger brother, Nathan, they did what people thought couldn't be done. They hit "Greektown Johnny" Salvatore. His name represented everything illegal in the city of Detroit. From drugs, to extortion, he profited from it all. But his legendary luck was about to change. Hank and Nathan had other things in mind for the drug lord. They planned a major withdrawal from Greektown Enterprises. They knew that his drug business was vulnerable. They also knew he was virtually untouchable. But that didn't matter. The robbery of five of Johnny's crack houses would get his attention for sure. He would turn the city upside down, looking for those responsible. But it wouldn't do him any good.

They wouldn't be in Detroit.

They'd be gone.

For good.

His brother had everything figured out. Sometimes, his compulsive attention to detail wasn't so bad, Hank thought as he reflected on how he hated that part of his brother when they were kids. He smiled, thinking about that and how Nate had never let them down before. Thinking about of all the money they'd soon split brought an even wider grin to his face.

Hank's smile left his face as a knock came, loud and hard, at the apartment door. His nerves exploded in the form of sweat as perspiration covered Hank's body immediately. His heartbeat rivaled that of a jackhammer in action.

"YEAH, WHO THE HELL IS IT?" He hoped he sounded very pissed off.

"Yo, man, I got a message for Hank."

"OH YEAH? FROM WHO?"

"Hey, blood, you want me to shout it out, no problem."

"WAIT A MINUTE," he replied, trying to steady the quiver in his voice.

Hank waited a moment before he made his way to the thick wooden door. He cursed himself for not having a peephole installed, like he had planned to do for months.

"Calm down. Be cool," he muttered.

As he gripped the doorknob, the sweat began to roll down his forehead. Why had he let Nathan talk him into this shit? He knew when they left the last house that something had gone wrong.

He opened the door slowly, one hand on the trigger of his .22 caliber pistol.

Standing on the other side of the door was a tall, skinny, kid. He stood maybe 6'5," but no more than 170 lbs. He looked like he should be at home, dreaming of girls and basketball instead of delivering messages at two o'clock in the morning.

"So what's the message?"

"Inside, man."

Hank stepped back and let the kid in. He could be no more than fifteen.

"It's from Nathan. He needs to see you."

"What do you mean he needs to see me?"

The tall, skinny kid looked at Hank with a puzzled look on his face.

"They said you'd know what that meant."

"Who is they?"

The kid shrugged his shoulders with an "I don't give a fuck" attitude that Hank didn't appreciate.

"I dunno."

Without warning, Hank grabbed the boy around the collar and spun him around, slamming him face first into the door.

"HEY, MAN. WHAT THE HELL YOU DOIN'?" The boy was scared now.

"Look, young boy, I ain't got no time for no guessin' games. You got a message for me, let's hear it." Hank pushed the boy's arm up his back. He couldn't take a chance on who this kid was.

"HEY, DOG, CHILL. I GOT NO BEEF WIT YOU. I'M JUST A DELIVERY BOY, YOUKNOWHATIMSAYIN."

"Then deliver, motherfucka! I'm through playing with you. START TALKING!" Hank applied more pressure. His ability to lift massive amounts of weight, which he did twice weekly at the YMCA, guaranteed an imminent break. Ligaments in the arm began tearing.

"Okay. Okay," the youth pleaded, his voice rising. "Let go of my arm and I can give it to you." Hank backed off from the youngster, allowing him to reach in to his pocket.

"Easy now," Hank warned the boy, his right arm cocked back, his fist ready to do extreme damage to the youngster's face.

"I ain't gonna try nothing," the boy promised. The kid handed Hank a crumpled piece of paper.

"They said you would know what this means. Can I go now?" his voice trembled.

"Shut up," Hank replied harshly.

His interest was on the paper.

"Go sit down. Don't move until I tell you to."

The kid stood there, rubbing his arm, tears clouding his eyes. He slowly made his way over to the chair in the corner of the room.

Hank went over to the table and sat down. His hand was trembling again. This was bad. He could feel it. As he unfolded the paper, he could feel the weight of something in the ball of paper, about the length of a roll of pennies, only not as heavy. As he unwrapped the paper, he could see the object was wrapped around a bill.

"What the hell . . . " Hank mumbled, still unsure of the contents.

Inside the paper, wrapped neatly so that the excess blood wouldn't run out, was the ring finger of a man. It was wrapped in five $100 bills.

*　　*　　*

Jeri Day found herself unable to sleep this early morning as her thoughts kept drifting back to the events of the previous day, with Nathan being so sweet and mysterious.

"I'm gonna give you the world, baby. I got me a deal going that's gonna get us some real money so we can start livin' right, youknowhatImsayin? After tonight, we gonna be straight." He kissed her gently on the lips. "Wish me luck."

And with that, he was out the door. She hadn't talked to him for the rest of the day, and now, it was already 2:00 A.M. and still no word from him. She rose from her restless night, still excited. She wished Nathan were there right now. She had so many questions about this latest deal. This wasn't the first time Nate had some sweet deal cooking, only to have it blow up in his face. Still, he was acting different this time. Hopefully, it won't be a scheme, like with that water purifying company.

"This is going to be the rage of the 'nineties," he told Jeri about this earlier attempt at instant wealth. After hearing that a retired pro football player from the city had invested, Nathan jumped on the bandwagon. The company was looking for local investors and the job he had at TEZ Automotive was a dead-end, so he was ready to make a move. He was always hustling on the streets, supplementing his income with the nickel-and-dime amount of cash he got by selling weed. The money he made selling marijuana was small compared to what he could make by being in on the ground floor of a big-time operation. Unfortunately, the majority of the boards of directors of the bogus water company were indicted for running the pyramid scheme and Nathan lost all his money, something that Jeri didn't let him forget. But that was then. This is now. And now, he was promising her the world. She couldn't wait to find out what Nathan Littlejohn was up to.

*   *   *

Nathan Littlejohn was feeling on top of the world as he cruised down Woodward, checking out the streets. They were full of people hanging out, still trying to find some excitement before heading home. Excitement was something he had no problem finding that morning. He was riding the high of adrenaline as he replayed the events of a couple of hours ago over in his mind. After gaining access to the first drug house, it was no problem subduing the weak security "Greektown Johnny" employed. They weren't made men, just nickel-and-dime hustlers the mob used. Stringing them along to make them feel like part of "the family" allowed the mob to have the necessary faces of color needed to be successful in the inner-city neighborhood. Those who worked for "Greektown Johnny" didn't have the balls to fuck with the mob's money.

What Johnny didn't count on was the fact that even if they wouldn't fuck with his money, most of them didn't care if someone was stupid enough to attempt a hit on the mob. They figured nobody would be insane enough to try that again. Not after the last time. Nathan, Hank, and Jenks heard the story, like everyone else. Three crackheads tried to rush one of Johnny's houses one night. They had no real plan or any real idea what they were doing. Desperation, plus a crack monkey on your back, makes you do stupid things. What they didn't know was that it was pickup night so there were heavy hitters in the house collecting. That was the first house on the list. Their bad timing was crucial.

The crackhead's bodies were found in the Detroit River, "old school" style. Kneecaps busted, fingers broken, feet in buckets of cement. That was two years ago. Since then, the mob has gotten sloppy. Nathan watched and waited and planned. Jenks was so well known as the local dope fiend, his involvement in a robbery would hardly be questioned. Once Nathan convinced Jenks that he wouldn't be suspected, it was clear sailing. So it was on.

Nathan made sure that they hit quickly before Johnny had a chance to realize what was happening. Once inside the dope house, the two faceless men, brandishing automatic weapons, would subdue the weak security, who would offer little resistance. The story was the same at the next three dope houses. Wait for Jenks to get inside. His deal would take no more than five minutes, eight tops to make his purchase and be on his way out. When that door opened, bum-rush the weak-ass security, tie them up and throw them in the basement. Flush all the dope they could find, take all the cash and split. It was different at the last place. A couple of hoods rolled up on them as soon as they came out of the house. Somehow, they must have been tipped because there was no hesitation in their actions. They started blasting immediately. Hank and Nathan returned fire, with Hank hitting one of the shooters in the midsection with his .45 automatic. The other one pulled him in to their car and took off.

That changed their plan slightly.

Instead of lying low for a couple of days, they needed to leave now. After flying down I-94 in what seemed like two seconds, Nathan got Jenks to his house. Then he and Hank went their separate ways. They would make contact again when they hit Vegas. After a couple of calls to make sure their way out of town was secured, he'd swing by Jeri's, pick her up, then be on their way. Then he saw her.

It must be fate, he thought vaguely as he slowed down. There were three women and two men outside of RJ's party store. One of the women was tall, about six feet and well put together, like she worked out twice a week at Vic Tannys, which she did. *An ebony princess*, Nathan thought. One was a white, older woman. She looked as though she'd been on the streets too long. The third was a youngster, a fair-skinned girl who came from a mixed union in which she inherited classic beauty. She was tight, but the ebony one was who he needed.

As he hit the ever-present joint in his mouth, he realized she had spotted him. That's why she started performing. He smiled, recalling their last time together. It was weird seeing her, tonight of all nights, he thought, inhaling deeply.

Kay Brown shot a quick peek over her shoulder at the man who just pulled up, and smiled. She knew what that meant. Time to get laid. It had been a while since the two of them were together. Did this mean he finally broke up with his stiff-assed woman?

"Come on baby, what's up?" one of the men blurted out, interrupting her thoughts. "You gonna go over to Tyrone's to see if he's on or what." one of the men said.

"Listen, man, you'd be better off walking your lame ass up the street than fucking with me," she said with disgust. She was in no mood to go and score some coke for this dude.

"Go on, creep, keep steppin'," the white woman piped in.

"Fuck you, bitch. Me and the girl had a deal. Now, you callin' the man or not?" he pressed.

The cokehead's partner was getting nervous. He kept looking at his watch.

"Come on, man, we gotta go. You can get that shit later," he stated as he started off down the street.

"You better listen to your boy," the "ebony princess" advised.

The other man waited for a second, turned and looked at the three women, then followed his partner. Before fading down the street, they could hear the man in the distance.

"I'LL BE BACK. COUNT ON IT."

Nathan watched the scene from his car and he smiled. She was showing him how tough she was. He was sure of that. One thing Nathan knew was people. He was an excellent judge of character, women in particular. Not many take the time to study people the way he does.

He checked his watch. He was running late. His plans with Jeri would be put on hold for now.

"So, you through with your business or what?" he yelled out the car window.

She looked at Nathan with a roll of her eyes. She made no move to show him she was interested. But he knew this game, and he played it with the best of them.

"Enough of this bullshit, I'm gone." With that said, he started the engine.

"Wait, I was just teasing," she turned to the others who were still laughing at the way she dogged that wannabe player.

"I'll see ya'll later. I got me a date tonight."

"Well, go head with your bad self," the young girl laughed.

"Got room for one more?" the white woman inquired.

"Sorry, baby, this is one on one tonight," Kay replied, opening the passenger door of the Mustang.

Kay hopped in the front seat and smiled at Nathan.

"You know you were on my list, don't you?" she leaned over and blew softly in his ear.

"What list?" he asked as he pulled into traffic, cutting off the car coming up behind him. "My shit list. You haven't been coming by or calling for weeks, and now you just ride up at two in the morning and expect me to drop everything and run off with you to some motel."

"Hold it!" he jerked the car over suddenly.

"What makes you think that I wanted to take you to a motel? I might just want you to blow me right here," he said coldly.

She gave him that look that only black women can give. "Ain't that a bitch? If you think you can just ride down on me like some kind of whore, that you can go fuck . . . "

Kay Brown couldn't finish because the sound of screeching tires made her jump in her seat. Nathan turned, his hand reaching for the 9 mm berretta under his seat. His mind was racing wildly. Maybe something had gone wrong.

"HEY MOTHAFUCKA! YOU GOT A DEATH WISH OR SOMETHIN'? YOU ALMOST FUCKED MY CAR UP!"

It was the driver of the car Nathan cut off a few minutes before, a young boy trying to impress his even younger girlfriend. She was not looking impressed, but scared.

"Come on, Jason, let's go. Don't start no trouble," the girl pleaded.

"YEAH MAN, YOU BETTER LISTEN TO YOUR GIRL," Nathan shouted back to the young boy. He was in no mood for this bullshit. He was wasting time if he wanted to get anything done before he hooked up with Jeri.

"Fuck that! That nigga pulled in front of me and almost sent you through the windshield and you're tellin' me I'm startin' trouble. Shit, you haven't seen trouble yet," the young boy said bravely.

Nathan looked at his watch and knew this couldn't go on. He had to get off the streets.

"Look, dog, take your punk ass home before your girl sees me put these Nikes up your ass."

With that, he pulled the gun from under his seat and pointed it at the boy's face. "NOW, GET THE FUCK OUTTA HERE!"

The sound and smell of tires burning rubber once again filled the air as the car with the young boy and his girl took off down the street, almost sideswiping a parked car in the process.

"Nathan, are you crazy?" Kay asked, forgetting her anger moments ago.

He had begun to wonder the same thing. When they finished the last crack house, they agreed to keep low profiles and get off the streets. Nathan had a few loose ends to tie up before pulling out and dealin' with this crazy chick was on his list of things to do. He must be crazy. But he had to make sure she would be quiet. Kay was sometimes around when Hank and Jenks came by his apartment in Palmer Park when they were in the final planning stages. He had to make sure she didn't know anything. Pulling out that gun was a stupid move, he thought, but he knew he could cover that up. But Kay Brown wasn't stupid. She could put two and two together quickly. If she figured out what they did tonight, it could be trouble. She had a big mouth. If Nathan Littlejohn were a little more aware, he would know that trouble was exactly what was headed in his direction. Trouble in the form of a black sedan. The same dark sedan that made a delivery to Hank's place less than one hour ago.

CHAPTER TWO

Hank felt his insides being torn apart while the meat grinder they were in was set on high speed. That's why he couldn't get Jenks at his house. Someone had gotten to him first. All of the planning they did meant nothing now. Someone caught up to Jenks, and now, he was missing. How did they find out so fast? Was Jenks careless? He likes to get high, and when that pipe started callin' his name, Jenks was through. Maybe he got picked up. Shit, who knows? That's what can happen when you depend on a crackhead.

All these thoughts flooded Hank's mind a split second before he decided his next move.

Hank looked down at the boy. He was still looking scared, like he knew something bad was about to happen. He was very perceptive.

"Look, man, I need to get out of here. I got to get home before . . . " Before he could even finish his sentence, Hank grabbed him and pulled him out of his chair.

"YOU AIN'T GOIN' NOWHERE, DOG, UNTIL YOU TELL ME WHAT I WANT TO KNOW. WHERE DID YOU GET THIS?" Hank shoved the bloody finger in the boy's face. "You better start talkin', young blood, with the quickness."

The boy started to say something before the contents of his stomach came rushing out, catching Hank full force on his shirt.

"SHIT!" Hank looked down at his vomit-covered FUBU jersey. "GODDAMN." He pushed the scared teenager back down in his chair, and then carefully pulled the ruined jersey over his head, dropping it on the floor.

"You start talkin'," Hank said, staring at the frightened youngster. "Or I'm shovin' this finger down your throat and pulling it out your ass."

As the muscles on his LL Cool J type physique twitched, the boy needed no further inducement. He started singing like a Motown superstar.

"Hey man, I don't know anything. I was goin' to the store when these two white dudes asked if I wanted to make a quick ten. I said, 'hell, yeah,' and they gave me that package and told me to bring it to this address and say it was from Nathan. That's it, man. That's all I know. I swear that's it."

Hank looked down at him and knew he wasn't lying. He was too scared to be hooked up in all this bullshit. But he needed more information. Maybe he was playing the wrong angle in this. He studied the boy for a minute, then decided to play the good guy role. The bad guy did nothing but get his FUBU fucked up.

"Okay, kid," Hank said calmly, "I don't wanna give a young brother like yourself a hard time, but you've got information that could be dangerous to your health. These dudes that gave you the package, how long ago did it happen, and where?"

"I told you man, at the store down the street. Petey J's, on the corner. About fifteen minutes ago," the boy added.

"They gave you my number?"

"Nope, they asked me if I knew where the Madison Apartments were and I told 'em I'd find your address for that young ten."

Hank looked at the boy for a minute before he knew what he had to do.

"All right, kid, everything's cool. I didn't mean to come down on you that tough."

The boy was relieved to see Hank calm down. He felt easy for the first time since entering the apartment, except for his arm hurting like hell.

"That's all right. I can handle it. We cool? Can I book? I got my own problems," the boy said.

"What's your name, man?"

"Sharrod."

"Where you from?"

"Westside."

Hank looked at the boy and thought this kid don't know shit. If he had any idea what was goin' on, he wasn't showin' it.

"All right, Westside, get on up. I got things to do. I'll be seeing you around."

Sharrod looked at Hank for a moment before he made his way to the door.

"Hold it, kid."

Hank tossed him a towel from the couch.

"Clean yourself up. And stay out of trouble. You ain't ready to handle the shit you getting into."

"All right, old school, I'm out," he said, wiping his mouth. "You won't be seein' me no more." He handed Hank the vomit-stained towel, and out he went.

After watching the young boy disappear down the stairs, Hank took the vomit-covered jersey and threw it down the trash chute. Going back to his apartment, he went to his bedroom, where he grabbed another shirt. As he slipped it over his head, he inadvertently knocked over the weed tray sitting on top of his dresser.

"FUCK!"

Staring at the spilled marijuana on the floor, he decided on his first move. He had to find his brother. If they found him this easy, then everybody involved was fucked. They got to Jenks first, and now they're on to him. He thought about the plan. As perfect as they thought it was, it was obvious something went wrong. He picked up a cocktail off the floor, found his lighter, grabbed his phone, and pushed the buttons.

"Be home man," Hank pleaded into the phone.

*   *   *

Nathan was starting to relax after his little run-in. He felt back in control. Kay was starting to relax herself. He knew what was coming next. She would be dropping hints about them going to eat. This was an eating woman. But he didn't mind. After the vodka and cranberry started kickin' in, he knew they would be on to the motel.

"Say, girl, fire up the 'J' in the ashtray."

"Yeah, I was waitin' for you to light it."

"I know you was. I seen your eyes as soon as you got in. It's some good shit too."

Kay put the joint under her nose.

"Yeah, boy. That's what I'm waitin' to inhale."

Suddenly, his pager went off, filling the air with that annoying beep.

"This is not the time for interruptions. It's the time to be gettin' that groove on," she stated.

Kay lit the joint and hit it a couple of times before passing it to Nathan. The car was now flowing with weed.

"Damn," she said, choking, "this is some good shit."

"No doubt," Nathan said, looking at his pager.

He frowned as he looked up and down the street for a pay phone. There was never a phone around when he needed one. And when there was one, it was usually busted.

"What you need to do is get you a cell phone," Kay said, reading his mind. "That way, I can call you when I need you, honey."

"I've thought about it. If I do, I won't be givin' my number out to everybody I hang with. That's not my style."

She looked at him for a minute, then smiled slowly. Her eyes were low and seductive.

"You not boning everybody." She took the joint out of his mouth and put it between her thick lips. Then she rubbed his crotch.

"Are you?"

"Come on now," he said, getting hard instantly. "I only got one female that I hang wit, you knowwhatImsayin?"

Before she could reply, he pulled over and jumped out of the car. With the night he had, he wanted to have a quick roll with Kay. He could find out what she knows before he got caught up in business. He had a feeling that wasn't going to happen. They used to hang all the time back in the days when he was doing nothing but hanging out 24/7. Getting high all the time and partying got tired fast, but an occasional hot evening did him good.

"Shit," he said, slamming the broken phone, "Just once, I would like to find a working phone when I need one." He looked up and down the street as he walked back to the car.

"This is fucked up," he said, slamming the car door shut. "We going over to Jimmy D's so I can lay low and make a few calls. You got time?"

"I got no plans, I'm free as a bird.

He leaned over and kissed her lightly on her cheek.

"Cool."

The two men driving the dark sedan behind Nathan Littlejohn for the last few miles could sense his growing restlessness as he raced through the city. They've seen this before: a man panicking when they know the mob is after him.

If they knew the makeup of their intended victim, they would have known that he wasn't panicking, but they weren't interested in studying the tendencies of this man. They were instructed to follow him and observe. The time to maim and kill, which they were experts at, would come later.

Marcello "the Bear" Baldino, a man well known to the Detroit Police Department, the FBI, and anyone who's had the misfortune of being in debt to "Greektown Johnny" Salvatore, was driving.

"The Bear" was indeed a proper moniker for this huge man. At six feet five inches and over 300 pounds, he dwarfed most men. He was a monster who had no feelings of remorse when it came time to do his job.

"JESUS, BEAR, SLOW DOWN! YOU WANT HIM TO SEE US?"

That was the shrill, annoying voice of Angelo "Little Vito" Arbolino, a small man who resembled the Barney Fife character from the old Andy Griffith show. At five feet four inches and 120 pounds, the irritating little psychopath resented anyone over six feet tall.

"Fuck you, Vito," came the standard reply. Needless to say, "Little Vito" loathed working with "the Bear." Their boss, who also stood well over six feet, found "Little Vito's" preoccupation with size amusing. But he was an expert in the field of torture and his various ways of extracting information from the most unwilling of participants made him invaluable to "Greektown Johnny." "Little Vito" Arbolino had a particular fetish for dismemberment.

The large man bit into a greasy Italian sausage he was eating, spraying a line of grease across the car, hitting Vito in the chest.

"Shit. Watch that . . . "

"IDIOT," Vito exploded. "YOU GOT GREASE ALL OVER ME!" He started wiping his shirt frantically with one of many newspapers that always littered the back seat. That only made the stain worse.

"Shit. This is fucked up. I can't go to the club like this."

"The Bear" was amused to see Vito trippin' about his shirt. He took pride in always being meticulously dressed. But now, his sweet Giorgio was ruined. The large man chuckled beneath his breath.

"After we handle the kid, we'll go by your place so you can get changed."

"Shit. This is fucked up," he repeated. "Why don't you watch what you doin'?" the little psycho whined.

"Okay, I got the message, all right?"

"Yeah, yeah."

The gangsters stayed three car lengths behind the Mustang carrying the unsuspecting couple. The cars moved along Woodward at a deliberate pace. Suddenly, the Mustang pulled over.

"All right, Marcello, pull over behind that van. Looks like he's goin' into that bar." Nathan pulled the sports car in front of the small building that housed Jimmy D's. There were images of the great jazz singers and musicians painted on the front, a faint reminder of the glorious past. That was just a distant memory of a better time for this location. Now, it was just one of many bars that littered the city. "Shit, I hate goin' into them nigger bars."

"Don't worry about it," Marcello said. "I'm on this."

Vito turned and looked at the huge man sitting next to him. He was relieved that his partner volunteered. It saved him the trouble of trying to manipulate Marcello, which he did frequently. "Little Vito" wasn't trying to go someplace where he was made to feel inferior, which always happened when he was in the company of blacks. Past his momentary inferiority complex, he returned to his usual foul personality.

"Oh yeah, you cool with the bros," he said in his feeble attempt to sound black.

"Yeah, we cool. I never have no problem when I got to deal with them."

"The Bear" pulled a comb out of the breast pocket of his sports coat and began combing his thick gray mane. "I'll tell ya something else," he said, looking into the rearview mirror.

"What?"

"You repeat this and I'll fuckin' kill ya."

"WHAT?"

"I got me a black girlfriend. Well, she's not really my girlfriend. She's somebody I . . . "

"What the fuck you talkin' about?" "Little Vito" interrupted. The little killer was stunned. "You ain't got no black girlfriend!"

The man called "the Bear" laughed at his partner's hostility.

"What, you think you know everything about me and what I do? Bullshit. You don't know shit about my personal life. We just do our fuckin' jobs and go about our fuckin' business. But that's how I like it."

This was one of the rare times Vito had no smart comeback to throw at his partner.

So he went back to business.

"He just went in. The broad went with him." Vito looked at his Rolex. "Almost two thirty. He's got an hour to lead us to his place."

"You think he knows about the present we gave his brother yet?" Marcello asked.

"It don't look like it. He looks pretty relaxed right now. Maybe he's gettin' ready to go fuckin' after he leaves here."

Vito sat back in the seat and lit a cigarette.

"Guess he ain't gonna get that pussy though."

Then the slightly crooked smile that showed the little psycho's $10,000 worth of bridgework flashed. "Hey, Marcello, maybe after we take care of him, you can go get wit your black bitch."

"The Bear" stared straight ahead as he replied.

"Fuck you, Vito."

CHAPTER THREE

Jimmy D's was jumping as usual. The crowd was always in and out, packed together like sardines in a can. But with the drinks they serve and the women who partied there, Jimmy D's is easily the most popular bar on the west side. It didn't hurt that some of the best connections for drugs were made at this establishment. A direct line to the best dope in the Motor City could be had for the right price, if you knew the right people. And those people had to know "Greektown Johnny."

"Hey, baby, what's happenin'?" Nathan called out to the bartender, a physically endowed woman named Jo, who loved all the attention her 42 double D's afforded her.

"Nathan Littlejohn, you better bring your fine ass over here and give me a hug."

She leaned over the bar and gave him the welcome sight of cleavage for days.

"Still got the best pair of tits on the west side," he smiled.

"You know somebody on the east that can get with me?" she said in mock anger.

"Hell, naw, I ain't goin' there," he laughed as she hugged him tight, ignoring the woman standing behind him. Kay didn't care. She was busy eyeing the room to see if she spotted a quick hustle from some unsuspecting loser. There was always a sucker around when you needed one, her experience taught her. She needed some cash, she thought as she pulled a cigarette from her purse. "I'll be back, baby. Goin' to pee."

With that, Kay Brown turned and looked over to a table where three men were sitting. She saw them as soon as she entered the bar. One old guy and what appeared to be a younger version of him, and an even younger version of the middle guy. Must be three generations, she thought as she sized them up. They seemed to be celebrating something, she figured as she caught the tale end of their conversation. Just then, "young guy" pulled out a pack of cigarettes. She waited until he pulled out one to light when she made her move. She'd done this move hundreds of times.

Straight out of *To Have or Have Not.*

With the quickness and grace of a feline, she strolled over to the table where the three men sat. In the blink of an eye, she leaned over, grabbed the man's wrist and put the flame from his lighter under her cigarette instead.

"Thank you." The three men stood up, while "middle-aged guy" extended her a chair. They were obviously pleased that she chose their table to explore.

"Young guy's" lengthy glance down her loose-fitting top, along with her sexy smile, guaranteed drinks for as long as she wanted. Lauren Bacall would have been proud. She looked over at Nathan. He was already on the phone. When he was done with his business, they would be off to the motel. She smiled, thinking about the next hour.

*   *   *

Beep beep beep . . . The piercing sound of Jeri's pager shook her awake from her nod.

"What time is it?" she wondered aloud. She looked at her clock, then sat back on the couch. Who was paging her at 2:30 in the morning? It better be Nathan. He should have been here by now. She picked up the pager off the coffee table and looked at the message. 313-197-6522-111.

"Why is that girl pagin' me at two thirty in the morning?" She looked at her pager again. Triple 1's was her sister Tia's code. Why didn't she just call the house?

Jeri got up and went to the bathroom. Just as she sat down, the phone started to ring.

"Damn. That always happens."

Knowing she had her answering machine on didn't keep her from wanting to jump off the throne and run to the phone. She didn't like messages. She liked contact. It's easy to back out on a machine. Suddenly, Nathan Littlejohns' voice filled the air.

"Hey, baby, what's happenin'? Something came up. I don't know how long it's going to take. You must be asleep. If it's not too late, I'll call you back. Or I'll see you tomorrow. Later." Click.

"Well, I'll be damned," she cursed.

After a few minutes, she left the bathroom and went to her bedroom, where she sat on the end of her bed. Turning on the 12-inch TV, she hit the remote and lay back, waiting for the onslaught of infomercials. To her surprise, *Starsky and Hutch* faded on. She leaned across her bed to the table, where she kept a mini-fridge. Reaching inside, she took out a beer. Sipping a brew and watching cable wasn't what she had in mind for the night.

After another surf of the 75 cable channels, she decided to stick to the Cartoon Channel. *Johnny Quest* would be on in fifteen minutes. She looked over to her phone and decided to call her sister back. Maybe she was ready to apologize. The last time they spoke, they ended up in an argument about Nathan. Tia didn't like him. She said Jeri was a fool to be with him. Now what could she want at 2:30 A.M?

* * *

Tia Day was a beautiful girl. With a 38-26-36 figure, she was a woman who commanded attention whenever she entered a room. Her light brown hair looked just right with the blond streaks, she thought, giving herself the once-over at the mirrored wall. At 5'8", 130 pounds, she's a couple of inches taller than her sister, but with the same light brown skin and high cheekbones. Whereas Jeri was a homebody, Tia felt she was missing something if she wasn't out hanging. She usually hit downtown, but her latest boy toy liked to hit the neighborhood clubs. He was at the bar, trying to get another round before last call.

That's when she saw Nathan Littlejohn come into the club with that bitch Kay Brown behind him. She knew he was still up to no good.

She tried to warn her sister, but she wasn't tryin' to listen. And now her nigga walks in with his ex.

She would listen this time.

"Hey, baby, you ready to go?" It was her latest, Sonny. He was buzzed and ready for his sexy girlfriend.

"Damn, Sonny, you just got back with the drinks," she replied. "Sit down."

He sat across from her at their table, blocking her view of the bar.

"No, honey, don't sit there," she said, sliding out the chair next to hers. "Sit here."

"All right, whatever. Let's just drink our drinks so we can go."

He worked the day shift at Jefferson's Stamping and he had to be there at 6:00 A.M. Why he was hanging at the bar this late was beyond him. But he had a hard time telling Tia no. She liked hanging and he wanted to be with her. It was that simple.

"Honey, can I use your phone for a minute? I need to make a quick call to my sister."

"Sure. Here you go," he said, handing her his phone.

"Then we're leaving, right? You know I gots to work in the morning."

She looked at him coolly for a minute as she listened to the busy signal.

"Busy. I need to page my sister and leave your number on the pager," she said, pushing the buttons. "That's not a problem, is it?"

He frowned.

"Of course not."

*　　*　　*

The cellular phone of "Greektown Johnny" rang, as he was about to sink his teeth into a thick T-bone steak. Like most of his underworld dealings, the steak was bloody. That's the way John Salvatore liked his steaks and his business. He enjoyed sending a message that left no doubt as to who was in charge.

"Yeah, what you got for me?" asked the mobster. "How long he been in there? He have anything with him? Shit, the dead nigger said he was supposed to be meeting his brother . . . That present, you delivered it? Good, good. Give the bastard time to have a couple of drinks. Check his car. The dumb prick might have our shit on him." He laughed as he jammed another piece of meat into his huge mouth.

"That finger should be motivation enough. If he don't know now we mean business, he ain't never gonna know. You don't see his brother in the next ten minutes, you go in there blastin'. I don't want nobody to walk away, you get me?"

He looked at an old couple across from him, who quickly averted their eyes from his table, obviously nervous.

"WHAT THE HELL YOU LOOKIN' AT?"

Another couple at the bar rose to leave. The old couple motioned for the waitress for their check. It was time to go.

"YEAH, THAT'S RIGHT. GET THE FUCK OUT OF HERE. ALL OF YA!"

The owner of Collazo's Restaurant came running from his office to find the long hand of "La Cosa Nostra" driving away his customers.

"HEY, COLLAZO! YOUR CUSTOMERS DON'T LOOK TOO HAPPY! WAS IT SOMETHING I SAID? HEY, I'M LIKE PACINO IN SCARFACE, EH? 'THE BAD GUY,' RIGHT?"

He laughed, debris flying out of his mouth.

Frank Collazo was a short, fat man. Standing five feet seven inches tall and weighing 255 pounds, he always looked hot and uncomfortable. He gave the impression that he was sweating all the time, even in the dead of winter. Frank Collazo was a man who didn't want trouble, but attracted it like a magnet. Maybe, his thirty-year association with "Greektown Johnny" made that happen. He's done his best over the years to resist being pulled into the mob life, yet it's at his restaurant where a lot of mob business gets done.

"Hey, Collazo, come over here," the mobster called.

Frank approached the table, cautiously hoping another outburst wasn't forthcoming. He needed twelve stitches for the last one.

"Yeah, John, what can I do for you?"

"What you can do is sit down and have a drink."

"I'm kind of busy in the back right now."

Johnny Salvatore didn't even look up from his dinner.

"Sit down, Frank."

He sat.

"Frank, you not still sore about that little pop on the head last week, are ya? That was nothing," the mobster laughed.

"What you got to understand is that I can't afford to look weak. Not for a second. You know that."

"Johnny," Frank started, "I don't know what you're . . . "

The words stopped suddenly as "Greektown Johnny" reached in to his jacket pocket.

"What's this?"

He threw an envelope on the table, waiting for an answer to his question. Frank looked at it for a moment before he picked it up. In thirty years, he's never been directly involved with any of Johnny's dealings.

"John," he began, "I really don't think . . . "

Out of nowhere came a backhand so quick and powerful that it took Frank Collazo completely out of the booth, sending him sprawling on the floor.

"Greektown Johnny" remained seated.

"Look in the envelope, Frankie."

Fumbling his way back in the booth, Frank wiped a small trickle of blood from his nose before he reached into the envelope.

"What's this?"

"It's called a videotape. A very handy machine called a videotape recorder plays those tapes. They also allow you to record things on them. Imagine that."

Detroit's number one criminal took a sip of wine before continuing.

"You can bet there's a lot of people who wish the VCR was never invented. Like those poor cops who were busted on tape, beatin' down that nigger a couple of years back. Or that sick bastard who killed that young girl and videotaped himself cuttin' her head off."

He cut another piece of steak and jammed it into his mouth.

"That's sick, ain't it?"

Was he kidding? Frank's overheard discussions about mutilations and killings that would give a serial killer pause.

"Ya know what's on this tape?"

Silence.

"Cat's got your tongue, eh? Tell you what," he said. "Let's go see it."

"John, I just can't leave . . . "

The mobster stood up abruptly, leaving no doubt as to his intentions. "I insist."

CHAPTER
FOUR

The ringing phone broke the silence. Hank Littlejohn took one more hit off the joint he was smoking, then answered.

"Yeah . . . well, we got problems. Big time . . . you don't want me to go into it now on the phone . . . Look, we gotta get together now . . . Look, man, we got busted . . . naw, I'm straight, but our boy ain't . . . I don't know all the details . . . I got a package a couple of minutes ago . . . yeah, it was pretty bad . . . Where are you? . . . Are you crazy? We're supposed to be keepin' a low profile . . . Yeah . . . If you seen what I seen you'd know he talked . . . Shit, I don't know. I haven't seen him since we split up . . . look, we can figure all that shit out when you get here . . . Well, . . . where then? . . . All right, I'm leavin' in a few minutes . . . Yeah, yeah, I know . . . Hey, I'm watchin' my back. You better do the same . . . later."

Hank knew all hell was going to break loose. How were they busted so quickly? They were very careful. No one knew of the plans.

Except for that bitch who was lurking around Nathan's apartment during the planning stages.

"I knew that bitch was trouble."

She was trouble all right. With a capital T.

"Look, ya'll, she's cool. She don't even know what's up, youknowwhat Imsayin? Trust me."

That's what Nathan told them when they voiced their disapproval of Kay Brown, always hanging around the apartment. And now it looks like it cost Jenks his life.

He took a long drag on the ever-present joint in his mouth. It was a long day and it was about to get longer.

"For you, Jenks. I hope you're still with us." His gut told him otherwise.

Nathan Littlejohn's evening was now ruined. After talking to his brother, he knew that the eye was on him and he had to make a quick escape.

What went wrong? Nobody knew nothin'. It was perfectly planned. He stood up, looking for Kay Brown. Where the fuck was she at?

"Shit. I gots to go," he said, standing from his barstool.

"Where you goin', man? You just got here," the buxom bartender sighed.

"Gots to go, baby. Business. You know how it is," Nathan said, looking through the crowd. "I'll get back."

That's when he saw her. On a cell phone. He knew by her face who she was talking to.

"Shit!" he cursed under his breath. "All right, Nate, be cool. You can play this off."

As he made his way over to Tia Day's table, his eyes were focused on hers, trying to read her face. He was pretty confident he could square things. It was bad being seen there with Kay Brown though. But worse was being seen there by a man whose job called for him to mangle, torture, and by any means necessary, enforce the rules of La Cosa Nostra. Over in the corner behind Tony, the numbers man and his partner, Big Andre, two frequent inhabitants of Jimmy D's, was that man.

And his eye was on Nathan Littlejohn.

It was 3:00 in the morning and Jeri Day was tired. Her body ached for sleep. She had been on the job since 6:00 A.M. and it was catching up to her. But she knew what she had to do. She had tried hard to forget what happened between Nathan and Kay Brown. But why are they together now? Tia could be a bitch sometimes, but she wouldn't lie about this. If they're together again after everything he's promised . . .

Her thoughts trailed off into a deep dark pit. All the promises and all the feelings of forgiveness vanished in a split second. Because she knew it was true. In her heart, she knew it was true. The thought of Nathan spending any time with Kay Brown was too much to think about. They had a future before she came on the scene. The thoughts were rushing at her . . .

Why? Why wouldn't that bitch leave him alone? Why couldn't he be stronger? How could he hurt her like this?

Didn't he think she'd find out?

Didn't he care?

She jumped out of her bed in a sudden rush, cursing as she threw things around her small bedroom, accidentally cracking the dresser mirror with her hairbrush.

"MUTHAFUCKINSONOFABITCH! HE THINKS HE CAN PLAY ME LIKE THAT?"

She went over to her closet and began moving clothes back and forth until she found what she was looking for.

In the back of her closet, on the floor, was a stuffed teddy bear. It was about 2 feet high, brown, with a tan face. It was wearing a hat and tie. Nathan won that for her at one of those traveling carnivals that come to the city every year. He had never won anything before that.

She smiled at the memory.

"This is our lucky bear," she remembered him saying after he sank the last of three long-distance shots to win the prize.

"With Mr. Yogi on our side, we got no worries."

Her smile faded with that memory.

"I got no worries," she said, looking at the smiling face of the bear. As she turned him on his stomach, she opened his back by separating a long Velcro strap. There was enough room inside Mr. Yogi that any number of small items could be put in there, maybe something that you wanted to hide. Money. Jewelry. Drugs. Reaching inside, she pulled out the only item she ever put in there: a small handgun. She looked into the cracked mirror, barely recognizing the cold eyes of the face that stared back at her through a hundred broken fragments.

"No worries at all."

CHAPTER FIVE

The dark sedan cruised down Woodward Avenue at a moderate pace. The driver has been on one of these rides before. He knew that the last thing his boss wanted was attention, and when you worked for "Greektown Johnny" Salvatore, you made damn sure he wasn't disturbed. He used to wonder why they called him "Greektown Johnny" when he first came to work for him. He wasn't Greek, but his hand was in all illegal moneymaking enterprises in and around the Greektown part of the city. Every restaurant, bar, and dance club owner had to pay him a weekly fee to belong to the Greektown Organization. The club was a thinly veiled extortion ring that guaranteed you protection from vandalism, although it was widely known that the damage was often provided by members of "Greektown Johnny's" family themselves. Between the full-time operations of his extortion, prostitution, and drug trafficking enterprises throughout the city, Johnny Salvatore had a hand in everything that generated money illegally. With all of Johnny's enterprises running smoothly, Frank Collazo thought Johnny wouldn't mind him missing an occasional payment. Considering all the mob business that gets done in his restaurant, it should be no big deal.

He was wrong.

The driver took a quick glance at Frank Collazo in the rearview mirror. He looked pale. And scared. Then the mobster in the back seat pushed one of the many buttons on a specialized control panel that did everything from shooting submachine guns from the rear lights, James

Bond style, to opening a side panel in the back seat, revealing a wet bar, stocked with the best and most expensive liquor.

This time, the button "Greektown Johnny" pushed turned on a voice activated tape recorder. It was a useful tool to have if you required accuracy from zealous media types, or if you were a celebrity prone to giving interviews. In the crime boss' dealings, he liked to record the cries of victims pleading for their lives for his listening pleasure.

"Well, Collazo," the mobster began, "I think you've done well for yourself. For thirty years, I've watched you build your restaurant up from a small home-cooking joint to a big-time operation, with pizza delivery all over the metro area."

The restaurant owner said nothing.

"You ever wonder why I started hangin' out, doing my business at your place?"

Collazo sat in silence.

"You had the store in the neighborhood where all the kids hung out. You know my kid, Nico, used to hang there at the store all the time, just like us when we were kids, eh? He used to come home running every day to tell me what was goin' on in the hood. It fascinated me. I began to hear things."

He leaned close to his passenger.

"I began to learn things." The crime boss pushed another button and the wet bar appeared.

"What'll you have?" he offered. "Here, have a scotch," he said, handing Collazo the drink. He poured himself one, sat back in his seat and took a sip of his drink. He savored his like a connoisseur.

"You know," the gangster began, "when my old man moved us here from New York, I was pissed. I was beginning to run the streets a little. You know nothing serious, just nickel-and-dime stuff. And he ups and moves the whole family to Detroit."

He took another sip.

"I thought my old man was gonna work in the auto factory. That's what he told us kids. And my mother never said nothin' to dispute that."

The way "Greektown Johnny" was going on and on about his past made Frank Collazo relax for a moment. He sat and listened and reflected on the old days when he and Johnny were pals. His family had just moved to Detroit from New York when he first met John Salvatore. He was about twelve or thirteen. The group of kids Frank hung out with didn't do too much in the way of trouble. Sure, somebody might snatch some fruit from the applecart or maybe skip school and go swimming off the pier. There were lots of things kids could do without getting into serious trouble. That is, until John Salvatore moved into the hood.

Collazo and his buddies used to hang out in front of his old man's sandwich shop. They would pass the time watchin' the cars drive by. There was always something going on in their block. If "Big Momma" Tessio next door wasn't breaking their balls about the amount of noise they generated, then his old man was bugging him about making deliveries around the neighborhood.

"You listen to me and you'll learn something," the older man was always telling him. "Home delivery will be big one day."

"Sure, Pop, sure," he answered as his father walked into his store, shaking his head, pondering his son's future.

That's when Frank Collazo first saw him.

"Hey, Frankie," little Tony asked, "who is that?"

"I don't know, Tony-boy," he answered. "Jimmy, you seen him before?"

"Nope."

"What about you, Mikey?"

"Never seen him before."

The four boys watched as a stranger about their age walked out of the apartment building across the street. Little Tony's apartment. The boy looked around for a minute before pulling a pack of cigarettes from his pocket and lighting one. The boys were astonished.

"Hey, Frankie, check that out," the boy called Mikey said.

"Hey, will you look at that."

"Check him out."

"He's smokin'."

"He's smokin'?"

"Smokin' what?"

"Cigarettes, stupid."

"Cool."

One by one, the boys announced how impressed they were with

the fact that someone their own age was cool enough to smoke out in the open. Although he too was impressed, Frankie kept his thoughts to himself. Frankie's father would kill him if he ever saw him smoking. So would the other boy's dads. Being raised in a strict Catholic household had its limitations. Still, the other boys looked up to Frankie. He wasn't their leader because it wasn't a gang, but it was obvious they valued his opinion. Rarely did they make a move without running their plans by Frankie.

"So what you think, Frankie?" began little Tony. "You think we should go see who he is?"

"Gentlemen, I believe we're about to find out."

As the boys were discussing him, he was busy checking them out. He had been on the block for a couple of days before he figured out who was who. Those kids seemed okay, from what he could pick up from the street. Because he's the new kid, he assumed he would get hassled, but so far, nothin'. He would find out who their leader was and before long, he would be making his mark in this neighborhood, like he's done wherever his family's moved to. He took another hit on the cigarette before tossing it to the ground. Now, to see where he fits in around here. As he made his way across the street, their body language, along with what he's heard, indicated that the storeowner's son seemed to be in charge.

The future crime boss approached the boys, extending his hand.

"Hey, how you guys doin'? I'm new in the neighborhood, but I guess ya'll know that already. I just moved in across the street a couple of days ago."

He flashed that killer smile of his that he would use in the future before going for the jugular.

"I'm John. But my friends call me Johnny."

The group hesitated, waiting for Frankie Collazo before responding. Frank looked at him for a moment, and then stood up.

"How you doin', Johnny?" he said, extending his hand. "The name's Collazo. Frank Collazo."

"How you doin', Frank?"

"Here, meet the boys of east Detroit. This here is Tony Caramandini."

"I live in that rat trap across the street too," Tony announced.

"That mug sittin' over there is Jimmy Brusca."

"What's up?" Jimmy greeted the newcomer.

"This is my partner in crime, Mike Garbarini."

Mike nodded.

Johnny flashed his killer smile.

"All right, I'm glad to get that out of the way. So tell me, what do you guys do for action around here?"

That was thirty years ago, before John Salvatore became "Greektown Johnny." It was difficult for Frank to believe that this man he now feared was the same person who extended his hand in friendship those many years ago. The sudden explosion of anger brought Frank Collazo back to the present.

"HEY. IDIOT," the mobster barked at the driver, "PULL THIS FUCKIN' CAR OVER NOW!"

The driver had his headphones on and was unaware that the crime boss had lowered the security glass. A violent slap on the back of the head changed that.

"PULL OVER, ASSHOLE!"

"Yeah, boss, sure thing," muttered the driver, rubbing his head.

The sedan pulled behind an old movie theater that was now a triple-X-rated live show. It was also one of "Greektown Johnny's" big moneymakers. They went to the back door, where a hulking brute answering to the name of Gino let them in. After whispering something in the brute's ear, the mobster motioned Frank to go upstairs, where his office was.

"I got a surprise for you, Frank. Upstairs."

The two men climbed the stairs, with Frank leading the way. Sweat began to bead up on his forehead as his mind began to race wildly. He was careful. He never got directly involved in John's business. Sometimes, John accused him of having a big mouth. He would have a little too much to drink and would say things he had no business saying. That's when he got those stitches. It was also when he decided he'd had enough.

"Go and sit down," the gangster ordered.

They entered the one-room apartment over the bar that doubled as the office. It was filled with the odor of stale beer and cigarettes. Dark and smoky, Frank could barely see two steps in front of him. In the corner sat four men, playing cards. He recognized three of the men. They've been at his restaurant a few times. He figured them for being members of the mob. The fourth man had his back to them. Frank couldn't see his face.

"Don't mind us, boys. Just goin' to watch a little TV," the gangster announced. They looked up for a minute and resumed their game. The room would light up from the flashing neon lights in the front. The lone window overlooked the street below.

"See that couch by the window? Park yourself on it. Watch some TV." He leaned over and put the tape in the VCR.

"I think you're going to enjoy this."

"Hold it, Johnny, I want to check this out."

That voice.

Frank Collazo knew that voice. From years ago, he knew that voice. He looked up. It was too dark to see across the room. It was the man whose back was turned to him.

Suddenly, the man stood up.

"You guys don't mind if we finish this later, do ya? My friend over there looks like he could use some company to watch this show, eh Johnny?"

"Yeah, I think so," laughed the mob boss.

As the man approached, Frank Collazo's eyes widened with a look of disbelief as he recognized the face that belonged to the voice.

"Hello, Frankie," the man smiled. He blew perfect smoke rings from his cigarette. "How ya been?"

Ordinarily, seeing someone from your past whom you grew up with, played stickball with, partied with, and chased girls with would be cause for celebration. This was no ordinary situation.

"Jesus. I don't believe it," muttered Frank.

"Believe what you see. It's me."

Standing before him was one of his closest friends before John Salvatore came into his life.

"I know what you're thinking. That it's impossible. That it couldn't be me."

He took a step closer.

"But it is me."

Frank Collazo stood up and faced Mike Garbarini for the first time in nearly three decades. Unbelievable.

"This is cause for a real celebration, eh?" the mobster declared. "After almost thirty years . . . "

"Twenty-seven years and four months," interrupted Mike. It got very quiet as the sounds from the street filled the room. Somewhere in the distance, a drunk called out for his lost bottle of wine. A couple outside the bar argued over the merits of going in to the club. In that small room over the club, drama was unfolding like a road map.

"Yeah, it's been a long time since the three of us were together," Mike continued.

"Do you remember the last time we were all together, Frank? I remember it like it was yesterday."

Frank couldn't look him in the eye.

"Come on, guys," said John. "We can talk about the old days later. Right now, I need Frank to tell me about some of my business."

"What are you talkin' about, John? You know I ain't involved in your business."

The gangland boss walked across the room to the lone desk and opened the top drawer. He pulled out a .45 caliber automatic pistol, the chrome gun shining in the dimly lit room. Johnny pulled a handkerchief and started wiping it tenderly like a newborn baby. After looking it over carefully, he walked back over to a visibly nervous Frank Collazo.

"You say you know nothin' about my business, eh?"

He pointed a remote he got from his desk at the TV/VCR.

"Then you tell me what this is about."

On the 27-inch TV screen appeared two men, talking. One was an old, black man. He was trembling, as if he had the shakes of an alcoholic. The other, a short, overweight, balding white man, kept looking around every few seconds as they spoke. They were in deep conversation at a bar.

"I don't believe it," said Frank, recognizing the scene.

The balding, sweating, nervous man on the screen was Frank Collazo, standing behind the bar, giving a drink to Mr. Samuel Jenkins.

"What I want to know," began John, "is what is goin' on between you and that nigger?"

The sweat's vacation from Frank's forehead was over.

"Nothin'. Just making conversation, that's all. How long you been spyin' in my place? I guess the phone's tapped?"

"What d'ya think?" the gangster replied. "I wasn't gonna keep tabs on you?" Out of nowhere came another one of "Greektown Johnny's" backhands that returned Frank's face color from pale to red. Blood followed its familiar path out his nose.

"Frank," the mobster began, "you know I'm not a patient man. When I ask questions, I want answers, not bullshit."

He looked at Mike.

"Get him a drink."

Mike crossed the room and went over to the wet bar, where a few half-empty bottles of liquor sat on top. He poured himself a drink before making one for Frank. After walking back over to the couch, he sat the drink in front of the pizza man.

"Watch the TV, Frank," Mike ordered as he downed his scotch.

The new image on the screen was revolting. It showed the image of another black man, tied to a chair. Sweat ran down his forehead to his stinging red eyes. Strapped around his head, into his mouth, was a rubber ball. It was forcing him to breathe through a recently broken nose.

Straight out of *Pulp Fiction*, Frank thought.

"You've been at my house before," the gangster began. "Been to a few parties, a couple of dinners." Johnny sat down on the couch next to Frank. He stared at the TV screen as he continued, fascinated by what he was watching. Frank stared at the gun in Johnny's hand. "At my last cookout, I remember you not mingling with my guests or even trying to seduce my wife, like most others."

The mobster let out a chilling laugh, as if he had figured out the joke which no one else got.

"No, what I remember about you at my last party is that I always saw you talking to the help."

He leaned closer to Frank's face.

"Specifically, my butler."

Frank swallowed what was left of his drink.

"Now a lot of people say it's politically incorrect to have a staff of black people working for you as maids and butlers and such. Hell, I'll tell you what. When they can prove to me that your blacks ain't the best at layin' my clothes out and drawing my bath and driving my car, that will be the day a lot of good black folks will be out on the streets."

John paused, like Johnny Carson delivering his monologue.

"My butler was a loyal servant. I was surprised to see him in your bar, having a heart-to-heart with you. It hurt my feelings that he didn't come to me with his problems," he said with mock concern.

The image on the TV was becoming unbearable to watch. Frank turned his head away from the TV, only to have the end of Johnny's gun force him to resume watching the horrific scene.

"I asked my butler if he had seen his son lately, but he was no help." The mobster smiled as he watched the TV.

Frank stared at the screen as the young man on the TV attempted a scream. A garbled sound was the best he could do. The rubber ball prevented much more. Suddenly, the man in the chair began squirming violently. The reason for his renewed desperation became apparent as the camera zoomed out. The ring finger on his right hand was being cut off with a pair of wire cutters.

"As you can see," the crime boss grinned, "I found him."

CHAPTER SIX

The way Nathan Littlejohn leaned over the table to greet Tia Day, he carried himself like he had no worries. In fact, his mind was racing in a thousand directions at once. He knew he had to meet his brother and get out of sight. First, to deal with . . .

"Tia, how you doin', girl?" he said, flashing a smile.

She looked him up and down before turning to Sonny.

"Honey," she said sweetly, "this is my sister's old man and we got some family business to discuss."

She looked at Sonny straight in the eye with a look he'd seen before.

Their night was over.

"You don't mind, do you?"

Taking his cue, he stood up.

"Hell, naw, baby, I don't mind," he lied. "I got to be up early anyway." Sonny looked Nate over before slamming his drink.

"Ahhh, that was good. Well, baby, you gonna be all right?"

She looked at Nate and smiled.

"Yes, I'll be fine," she said as her eyes never left Nathan's stare. Sonny looked troubled for a moment before regaining focus.

"All right, then, I'm out of here. I'll call you."

She gave him a totally disinterested wave of the hand.

"Mmm . . . hmm."

Now that she'd gotten rid of the pesky autoworker, she could turn her attention to Nathan. Tia Day looked her sister's boyfriend in the face and began her weak attempt at interrogation.

"So what's happenin', Nate? Surprised to see you here."

"Oh yeah?" he said, looking over his shoulder. "Why is that?"

Tia took a sip of the drink that Sonny bought her before his quick exit.

"I just don't see you out much anymore."

She smiled at him like the cat that swallowed the canary.

"Been busy. You know, with your sister."

His mind continued racing.

"You talk to her tonight? I called but she wasn't there."

"No, I haven't," she lied.

They sat in silence for a moment, both trying to outfox the other. Nathan scanned the room, finally spotting Kay Brown over in the corner at the DJ's booth. As R. Kelly's "Bump 'N' Grind" blasted throughout the club, the DJ known as "DJ Heat" had his hands exploring some of the intimate parts of her body while she sat on his lap. Kay Brown wasn't choosy about where she was when it was time to get her groove on. She could tell by the look on Nathan's face that he'd seen her. Nathan could tell by the look on her face that she was receiving some sort of sexual pleasure.

That bitch, he thought as he saw the DJ's hand move under her shirt to begin groping her breasts.

"So, tell me, Nate," Tia said, regaining his attention. "What exactly are you doing here with that bitch?"

He looked over at her for a moment before reaching over and taking her drink.

"Look, Tia," he said taking a sip. "I don't have to explain myself to you."

He leaned over, his face close to hers.

"But since you're my favorite girl besides your sister, I'll tell you."

As Nathan Littlejohn began lying to Tia Day, the huge assassin in the corner ordered another drink. He could barely see in the dark club, but when the strobe lights from the dance floor would flash, he could see the top of Kay Brown's head moving up and down behind the DJ's table in slow-motion effect. Behind the dark glasses was the look of a man thoroughly enjoying the fringe benefits to his job. He sat, grinning broadly.

"A lot of action in this joint," the professional killer said to himself as he downed the vodka. He glanced over at the table where Nathan and Tia sat. They were in deep discussion. *Guess he didn't mind his girl workin' the DJ*, the killer thought. The action at the DJ's booth got him thinking about his own girl. Although he didn't get a good look at the face at the DJ's booth, he appreciated the physical similarities between them. Maybe when this was over, he'd go to Pussycat's. It's been too long since he'd gotten laid. After business, he would check his girl out.

"The Bear" met his girl at Pussycat's, where she worked as an exotic dancer. After $100 in tips, he got her attention. Pretty soon, they were slammin' vodka faster than an alcoholic at an all-you-can-drink taste fest. He never met a woman who could drink and not get blown out, but she stayed with him, drink for drink. Soon after that, they arrived at a motel for the beginning of what turned out to be one of the most significant periods of the killer's otherwise lonely existence. Finding out he was a made man only added to her thrill.

"LAST CALL, PEOPLE! ORDER UP!" the buxom bartender announced.

"One more down here," the hit man motioned.

Jo, the bartender with the best pair of tits on the west side, brought Marcello Baldino his Absolut and cranberry.

His girl introduced him to that drink at the motel.

"Five dollars," the bartender said.

He pulled a fifty out of his wallet and laid it on the bar.

"Say, beautiful, can you help me?"

The fifty caught her attention.

This isn't another creep fascinated with my gifts from God, is it? she thought.

"Yeah," she asked. "What is it?"

"You know that guy?"

"What guy?"

"The one you were talkin' to a while ago. The one who came in here with that girl givin' head to the DJ."

Jo's head whipped around in a blur to the DJ's booth, just in time to see Kay Brown rising from her kneeling position.

'YEAH, BOYEEEE! WE GONNA PUMP IT UP!!!" the elated DJ screamed into the microphone.

Good head does wonders for the attitude.

"What are you, a cop?" she asked, her voice low, dripping suspicion. "I'm just the bartender here."

"Naw," he said, gazing into her massive cleavage, "I'm no cop. But they might be interested to know about the action in here."

He glanced over at the small-time numbers man and his friend, the loan shark. Tony and Big Andre recognized the huge assassin as soon as he entered, thanks to their many dealings with the "Greektown Family." They nodded their heads in unison, acknowledging his stare. Looking around the room, they knew that his presence meant trouble for somebody in attendance. One call to John Salvatore and kiss whoever goodbye.

"Don't worry," Marcello said as he took the fifty and reached over the bar and put it in her bosom. "These questions will not be painful."

She hesitated a moment before she answered him. "There's nothing I can tell you."

"Sure, there is. The guy I'm talkin' about has a brother. He's supposed to be meeting me here, only I'm not sure what he looks like and we got some private business to discuss. It would help me if you could point him out."

She looked worried, unsure of what to do.

"Why don't you go sit with his brother?"

He glanced over at Nathan Littlejohn, still lying to Tia Day over at the table.

"I think his brother wants to spend some time with his lady friend over there."

He took another long look into her cleavage.

"Besides, I believe in givin' a man his space when he's gettin' his game on, you know what I'm sayin'?"

She saw the look on his face. She liked the way he spoke. She could tell he'd spent some time in the company of brothas and sistas before. A new man hadn't satisfied her in a long while. Maybe, this was her time.

"Look, maybe we can go for breakfast or something . . . when you're done with your business, I mean."

She hesitated, trying without success, not to sound too desperate.

The huge killer knew he had her.

Suddenly, a face jumped out of the crowd at her.

"I hope your meeting will be over soon," she said, motioning to the door.

"His brother just walked in."

CHAPTER
SEVEN

The red 924 Porsche made its way down Woodward Avenue at a high rate of speed, fueled by the anger of its driver. Jeri Day didn't care that she had run two red lights, crossed the center line a few times, and caused one accident that she was aware of. None of that mattered to her. The only thing she was aware of was the time. She looked at the clock on the dashboard of the little two-seater. She knew Jimmy D's was closing and that if she wanted to get there in time to bust Nathan, she would have to increase her speed. She took another quick glance in her rearview mirror, checked her blindside mirror, and then punched the accelerator. The small car responded instantly. The few people still on the street turned and looked at the red car fly by. At 3:00 in the morning, most were on their way home after a long night of partying. Some were going to breakfast at one of the many 24-hour Coney Islands on the west side, and some were going to the after-hour joints. She was hoping to catch Nathan before he disappeared into one of the many blind pigs that he frequented.

He thinks he's goin' somewhere with that bitch, she thought. *Not hardly!*

You know how you can be so mad that a "don't give a fuck" attitude controls your common sense? That was Jeri Day before zooming past a parked police car on the corner.

"Shit!" Getting stopped by the police was not part of her plans. She slowed for a brief moment when she noticed they made no attempt to come after her. They didn't even turn on their flashing lights. She watched them in her rearview mirror make no move towards her. Guess they didn't "give a fuck" either.

That was strange, but she didn't dwell on it. She knew she didn't have a lot of time to get to Jimmy D's. She planned to catch Nathan's ass red-handed. Maybe, then, he would think twice about fuckin' around on her, she reasoned. He'd know that she had her eye on him.

If he saw her at the bar, maybe he wouldn't have enough time to come up with a convenient cover story. Nathan was a good liar. She knew how convincing he could be.

"Why am I chasin' down this man?" she wondered aloud.

Because whatever he's done, he was still her man. He belonged to her. And she planned to let him know it.

"Make up your mind and then go for it. Don't let nobody stop you from gettin' yours. Nobody."

His words rang in her head as she approached Jimmy D's. People were still coming out. Good, still open.

She glanced up the street and could see Nathan's Mustang parked near the corner. After a brief interlude, her anger returned.

I should go break his fuckin' windows, she thought.

She sat for a minute before deciding against that move.

Better to wait and catch him with his pants down.

She thought about the moment when she first laid eyes on Kay Brown. They were at a jazz concert of a friend of Nathan's. The musician grew up with Nathan on the east side of Detroit before Nathan's family moved to the west side.

Although they rarely kept in touch, Nathan was able to keep abreast of his friends' activities. He went on to play pro basketball for a couple of years before an injury prematurely ended his career. That would have devastated most athletes but he saw it as an opportunity to follow his dream. Now, here he was in a concert on the river with some of the biggest names in jazz.

Jeri could tell Nathan was impressed by his friends' determination to follow his dream.

Maybe, something would happen for Nathan to find his own destiny.

Duke Arrington was Nathan's friend from the past who surprised them by calling Nathan at home and inviting him and a guest to his concert that night. It had been at least ten years since he last talked to him. He got word to him after a game once at the Palace when he played with Sacramento. Now, he was on the phone.

"Yeah, Duke, it's great to hear from you, man," Nathan said with rare excitement in his voice. He turned to Jeri, who was standing next to him.

"Duke's inviting us to his concert at Chene Park tonight. I know you want to go," he smiled. Her mind went zooming. She had a million things to do to get ready for this concert.

"Nathan, I have to get Cheryl to do my hair," Jeri announced as she raced around the apartment, gathering her things. She was gonna look hot for this rare night out with her man. The evening started out smooth and easy. Duke Arrington put on a helluva show.

Intermission time! Drinks from the expensive concession stand were needed.

"I'll have a cognac and a vodka with cranberry juice," Nathan said to the bartender, a tall, sexy thing with the deepest dimples he'd ever seen.

"Coming right up," she said with a wink.

Looking around the outdoor music venue, he thanked God for blessing him with perfect vision. Time now for every warm-blooded, heterosexual man's favorite pastime, selecting "this evening's top, visually exciting female." There were a lot of good-looking women flowing about. Washington, D.C., L.A., even New York couldn't compare to the women Detroit had to offer. The finest women in the country, Nathan decided as he eyeballed the Motor City crowd. *Oooh, look at that sexy thing over there. Low-rise jeans and a low-cut halter top.* Next to the shrimp-and-lobster special at Red Lobster, that was one of Nathan's favorite combinations. *Whoa, check out that sexy six-footer. Hot!* There's nothing like a Motown summer, Nathan grinned. Detroit was a large city, but it could be turned small before you knew it. That's when fate decides to slap you upside the head. These thoughts invaded Nathan's mind because of a face from the crowd that demanded his eyes. Why does trouble always arrive in the form of a fine woman?

Nathan remembered the last time he was with Kay Brown. They

used to spend lots of time together throughout the city. Sometimes, they would bone outside in the park, just to add a little spice to their sex games. She would find a nice, smooth tree trunk that was just right.

After drifting into another zone, reminiscing about their last time together, Jeri's voice brought him back to the present like a bucket of ice water down the pants.

"Nathan."

She shook his arm, snapping him out of his daze.

"Nathan, the girl said ten dollars. Where's your mind at?" she inquired.

He turned his attention to the fine bartender. "What you talkin' about? I heard her. I was just counting my money," he lied.

He sneaked a quick glance back at where Kay was standing a moment before. Gone in a sea of faces.

"Come on," he said, dropping a couple of dollars for "Dimples" on the counter. "Let's get back to our seats."

He grabbed the drinks, turned, and abruptly went speechless.

That's because Kay Brown, looking finer than she had a right to, was standing in front of Jeri and Nathan. The sexy memories came flooding back into Nathan's penis. How long had it been? Four, five years?

"Whoa, Kay Brown," he said with a nervous grin. "How you doin', girl?" Should he hug her, like he would an old friend?

She answered that question for him.

"Heyyyy!" she said, throwing her arms around him. "I don't rate a hug anymore?"

He glanced at Jeri, standing off to the side, checking Kay up and down, frowning.

Trouble.

"Hell, yeah," he answered trying to perfect the act of hugging her and standing so their bodies wouldn't be touching too intimately, all the while not spilling his drinks. Kay wasn't havin' that, though. She grabbed him tight, causing instantaneous hardness. He glanced at Jeri, being thankful for the baggy jeans he wore.

Big trouble.

Kay knew she made the woman with Nathan angry. She liked that.

Like most women who used their physical gifts as leverage, it made her feel powerful. She gave him a little squeeze before letting go. His pants told her they'd be having fun together again. Soon.

"Nathan," she asked innocently, "Aren't you gonna introduce me to your little friend?"

Women are like that. After jump-starting his engine, she stepped back off the gas, like she didn't know her foot was on the accelerator at all.

Nathan, hoping Jeri wouldn't notice how sweat had taken occupancy on his bald head, turned and faced his angry girlfriend.

"Jeri," he said ignoring her death stare, "This is a friend from high school, Kay Brown." Friend? That even sounded like bullshit to Nate.

Jeri gave her the cold stare. Kay smiled.

A few thousand seconds went by before Nathan continued his self-destruction.

"So, Kay, what's up?"

"Oh, a little of this, a little of that. You?"

He shrugged his shoulders. "Same old thang. Trying to make that loot."

Nathan fought like Ali against Frazier to avoid looking at her magnificent cleavage. HEADLINES: ALI GOES DOWN. FRAZIER WINS.

Stalling for time, he thought about ordering another round of drinks when he realized he still held two glasses in his hand. He did wish they were doubles now.

"Come on, Nate," Jeri said, starting to walk away. "The show's starting back up." Her look told him she meant business.

Ignoring Jeri, Kay kept the conversation going. She stepped closer and lowered her voice, making it sound sexier than he remembered.

"You still sellin' those good trees?"

He smiled as he dug his hole.

"You know it. Still smokin' it?"

"When it ain't garbage," she laughed.

"Nathan, you coming?" Jeri's voice had that edge that said "Enough, nigga!" He turned and looked at her, embarrassed.

"I'll be right there, all right?"

Kay noticed the tension and smiled, her mission complete. Now, for the final touch. She reached into her thirty-eights and pulled out a card and handed it to him.

"That's my pager number. Call me when you get some good shit." She hesitated, looking at Jeri.

"If you can."

His mouth dropped open, waiting for some clever response to come out, signaling his coolness. Nothing happened. She winked and turned away.

"Nice to meet you," she said over her shoulder to Jeri as she faded into the crowd.

Nathan knew Jeri was mad and figured the next thing said would make or break the evening, as far as he could tell.

"Was that necessary?" He heard the question come out his mouth before his brain could stop him. Wasn't love grand?

"You going to tell me that bitch wasn't making a play for you right in my face?" she stated coldly.

"I told you we're old friends. She's not even my type," he lied. She stared at him.

"What?"

"You gonna keep that number?"

He looked at the card and then put it in the back pocket of his baggy Karl Kani's.

"Women buy weed too," he replied.

Wrong answer. And just like that, their evening was over.

"Take me home Nathan. Right now."

"Take you home? Now? You must be crazy. I ain't goin' nowhere but back to my seat."

Jeri gave him the famous "black woman" look. You know the one: lips pursed together tight, eyebrows raised, head gyrating loosely on the neck, like one of those bobblehead dolls everyone is crazy about.

Think Florence, the maid, sassing George Jefferson. That look.

"You think I'm bullshittin'? I'm not gonna go back in there," she announced, completing the look with the mandatory placement of her hands on her hips.

"FINE, YOU WANNA GO HOME? I'LL TAKE YOU HOME."

He didn't realize he was shouting.

"DON'T SHOUT AT ME, NATHAN LITTLEJOHN," she shot back. "I'M NOT TAKIN' YOUR SHIT TONIGHT."

Jeri was losing her cool but no man, not even Nathan Littlejohn, was going to dog her.

"ALL RIGHT, All right, just chill," he said calmly. He took one last glance, hoping to spot Kay. No luck.

"Let's get the fuck on," he grumbled.

In the background, the saxophone wailed on as the angry couple walked out to the parking lot in silence.

The radio ended her reminiscing quickly. "That was sax man, Duke Arrington, off the CD *Lover Man*. He's got a new one that hasn't hit stores yet, but when it hits, you can catch it here on 109.9 WBBT with me, Ricky Love."

Every time she heard Duke now, it reminded her of that stupid concert. It seemed like it was just yesterday. And now, Nathan was with that whore.

"Okay, fine. He wants to play me for stupid, his ass is in for some serious wakeup."

She reclined her seat, barely showing her braided head through the window. Reaching under her seat, she pulled out the small handgun. She pointed the barrel of the 9mm at the entrance of Jimmy's.

"I got all night to wait for his ass."

CHAPTER EIGHT

The neatly dressed psychopath sitting in the dark sedan looked up from the latest Stephen King to glance at a red Porsche zooming down the street. It went half a block before making a quick U-turn to park across from the bar.

"Somebody's gonna get hurt driving like that."

"Little Vito" glanced at his watch. It won't be long now.

"What the hell is Marcello doing? He must've seen the guy come in."

A few minutes ago, a man entered the bar matching the description of Nathan Littlejohn's brother. The killer couldn't be sure because most blacks looked alike to him. He did have a worried look on his face. Delivery of a mutilated finger would have that effect. He smiled, thinking about the crude surgery he had performed earlier.

Did they really think they were going to get away clean? John Salvatore had ears everywhere. It was a good plan, hitting five of John's dope houses in one night. But when you get caught, you got to pay the piper.

"Little Vito" looked out on the street. A couple of winos were hanging out in front of the bar, hoping to bum some cash for liquor. Strolling across the street were two hookers, looking to get busy. He glanced down at his shirt. The grease stain had dried and left a big spot on the front. Wiping it with that paper was a mistake, he thought, giving it a halfhearted wipe with a napkin he found in the back seat.

"No way am I going to the club like this."

The club was Inferno's, a high-class gambling casino across the river in Canada that, unknown to the governments of both countries, John Salvatore had a piece of. The boys would go there two or three times a week. "Little Vito" especially enjoyed the company of the Canadian women who frequented the place. His chosen profession turned them on, he discovered early in his life of crime. Something about his violent lifestyle appealed to them.

He thought about his partners' admission about his black girlfriend. It bothered him.

Normally, it wouldn't matter to him who Marcello was bangin', particularly since they didn't hang out together outside of work. But this news bothered him.

In his bigoted mind, his partner was making a big mistake that could never be corrected unless he asked for forgiveness. Still, he was curious.

As his mind filled with all the myths and lies that ignorance demands, he noticed another black man fitting the description they were given walk into the bar.

"Fuck!" he exclaimed. "It's a fuckin' impossibility to tell these mooks apart."

Vito pulled out his cell phone to give his boss an update, knowing that "Greektown Johnny" expected it. He learned long ago to keep Johnny satisfied. His violent streak surprised even him and he didn't want to be on the receiving end of one of his famous outbursts. He glanced across the street at the red Porsche as the phone continued to ring.

Still, no movement. The small assassin had no idea that the actions of a few hours ago influenced the driver of the red sports car. That knowledge may have made him pay closer attention to the occupant, but he was oblivious of any connection they shared.

Putting the car out of his mind, he returned to the horrors of Stephen King's world. Soon, "Little Vito" would be serving up his own style of murder and mayhem: As soon as he got their orders.

* * *

"Greektown Johnny" Salvatore, crime boss, extortionist, and one-time killer for the five families of La Cosa Nostra, was watching the face of a man he had known for thirty years tremble with fear. It is the look he has seen many times throughout his life. The first time he saw the look of stark fear was when he committed his first hit. His boss gave him the assignment of collecting from a local storeowner who refused to pay for protection. Everybody has to pay, or it made him look bad in the neighborhood, the boss told the youthful enforcer.

"If you do good, I'll make sure you get plenty of work," he promised.

Looking into the eyes of a man you know is going to be dead by your hands wasn't easy. After the first couple of times, he found that he began to enjoy the feeling of power it gave him. To be in the position of deciding how someone dies. It was a thrill, like your first big jackpot, your first big rollercoaster ride, or your first fuck. Soon, he liked execution better than sex. By the time he had risen through the ranks from soldier to capo in the local mob family, killing had lost most of its allure for him. The last murder he committed was by cutting the throat of his first boss while they were at Belle Isle, fishing. He had gotten soft and the word was he had to go. By then, Johnny Salvatore, little-known enforcer and thug, had become "Greektown Johnny," flashy gangster and big-time operator of everything illegal in the Motor City. He planned to keep it that way.

The crime boss walked back across the dimly lit room to his desk, where he sat and poured himself another drink. He looked at the scared man on the couch for a second before putting the glass of liquor to his mouth. *Maybe I'll pull the trigger for old time's sake*, he thought to himself, smiling.

Frank Collazo sat on the couch, wondering when the shit would stop raining down on him. The mob boss stood up.

Not yet.

"You know what, Frank? You would be amazed how much information a little cocaine would get you," John began.

"Especially when you mix it with a little heroin to give it that extra kick," piped in one of the card players.

That brought laughter from the small group of men in the room. All except for Mike Garbarini. He just stared at Frank.

"So how you feelin', Frankie?" Mike said. "John didn't fuck ya up too much, did he?"

"Hell, no," the gangster interrupted. "Frank's fine. I'm just foolin' around with him."

He walked over to the couch where Frank was sitting, and sat next to him, putting his arm around him.

"You know, Mikey," the godfather began, "Frank and me, we never got close. Even after the cops sent you away, we never got close. I know Frank never thought you would get thirty. He used to tell us all the time how if he could he would trade places with you."

Mike's stare intensified.

"Yeah, all the time," he said, turning his head towards Frank. "Didn't ya, Frank?"

"Yeah, yeah, I said it," he said, shaking loose from the mob boss' arm. He stood up like he was receiving a medal.

"And I meant it."

With that, Mike Garbarini, a man Frank Collazo once thought of as his closest friend in the world, punched him in the face, knocking him back to the couch.

"YOU'RE A FUCKIN' LIAR!" he shouted while Frank tried to stop the blood, again from his nose. The other mobsters in the room looked over at the confusion on the couch, before resuming their game.

"What do I got to lie for?" the injured man implored. "I tried to set the record straight. I did. But nobody wanted to hear it."

He wiped the ever-flowing trickle of blood from his nose with the sleeve of his jacket.

"It was easier for the cops to hang you with the rap than go and catch the real killer. You think I didn't go to them when I found out what happened?"

Mike looked down on him as Frank tried to clean his face. The crime boss was looking at both of them intensely, trying to see where the situation was headed. He needed Mike to believe him.

"Look, man," Frank began. "When you came to me that night at the apartment, I didn't know what to think. You were going on and on about how your old man caught you and Johnny smokin' in the alley and he took you back to your place where he started beatin' you again. You said he knocked you into the closet and when he came at you, you clubbed him with a hammer."

He wiped his eyes before continuing

"You said you thought you killed him. I knew you was just protectin' yourself. When I told you to turn yourself in, I figured they'd see all the bruises you had and would believe you."

The room was quiet except for an occasional horn blowing from the street below. The gangsters in the room had abandoned their card game and were watching the scene play out in front of them, a scene they've all seen before: A man pleading for his life.

"I know I should've went with you to the cops, but me and cops, you know, just don't mix."

Mike didn't say anything. He just continued staring at Frank.

"Anyway, Little Tony came and got me. He told me that you was in jail for killin' your old man. I figured you was just protectin' yourself, so the cops had no right to keep you there. I went there to tell them that."

"That's when they told me he was shot five times. I didn't know what to think then."

Michael stared at him for another second before he walked over to John Salvatore's desk and poured himself a drink. He turned the drink up and sat on the corner of the desk, looking out the window.

"You know what?" he began, "I used to sit and stare out my cell window for hours, wondering what the outside world was up to while I wasted away."

He fixed himself another drink.

"I used to wonder if you guys still were hangin' out in the old neighborhood, sittin' on the steps, drivin' old lady Tessio crazy. Then, when I realized all my boys said the hell with me, leavin' me in this hellhole to rot, I got smart. No more hopin' for the day when the screws realize they made a mistake. No more thinkin' I was gonna get sprung."

He shifted his gaze from the streets below back to Frank Collazo.

"I used to wonder what the hell happened to you. Why didn't you come to my trial and tell them what happened? You know I didn't shoot my old man. I hated him for what he did to me, but I didn't shoot him."

Frank was ashamed that he didn't try to do more for his friend over the years. Shit, he didn't try to do anything for him.

"Remember that time we was all in the alley hangin' out when Johnny showed us those guns he got from his old man? You remember Johnny?" Mike said, turning to the mobster.

"Sure, kid," replied "Greektown Johnny." "I remember."

I bet you do, Frank thought as the images of that day returned to his head. He hadn't thought about that day in years.

The gang was in the alley behind Miller's garage, their unofficial headquarters. Johnny had taken two guns from his father's arsenal in the hall closet and brought them down to the alley so they could shoot some of the many rats they shared the space with. They each took turns, displaying various degrees of success.

Little Tony took a couple of shots before he hit a rat jumping out of the trash can. Jimmy took four shots, sending the boys scattering once to avoid a ricochet. Thankfully, he gave up in disgust. Frank took aim and fired, surprising himself and the others, killing two of the three rats he shot at.

Even then, John Salvatore was a crack shot. After reloading the now empty pistol, he aimed and fired. A hit. He smiled at his new crew. Ready, aim, fire! Success! Another one. Three more shots, three more hits. He didn't miss one. Coming from the docks of New York, he had plenty of practice, he explained. Only Mike didn't take a turn.

"I don't like guns," he told the young guns. "My old man is always wavin' them around, like havin' a gun is what makes him a man."

They teased him about it for a while before easing up. When they were done, Johnny put one of the guns behind a loose brick in the wall. That way, he explained, they always had access for target practice, or whatever they needed it for.

"I didn't like guns then," Mike said, regaining Frank's attention. "And I really don't like them now."

He reached into his pocket and pulled out a .45 caliber automatic.

"I guess sometimes, they're just necessary to do what has to be done."

He looked at Frank intensely.

"Did you know that Johnny was the only one to come see me at Jackson?" he questioned. "I guess you didn't have the spare time, seein' you were so busy takin' over for your old man. And now, you got pizza places all over the city."

Frank turned and looked at the mobster, whose head swayed side to side in a "tsk, tsk, tsk," sort of way.

"Johnny's filled me in over the years. You know, who's still in the hood, who's married, who's still alive, shit like that."

He walked over to Frank, sat next to him and continued. Frank's eyes shifted to the gun in Michael's hand.

"You know, Frank," he sighed, "I was surprised to find out that you turned on Johnny the way you did. Workin' with the blacks to rip him off. Not a good move.

You should've stayed in the pizza business instead of branchin' out to rippin' off crack houses." Frank Collazo glared at the annual winner of the Detroit Free Press' criminal of the year award, who smirked.

"I told you before, Frank. Nothin' gets past me. You think you were smart, gettin' my butler's crackhead son to hit my dope houses with his crew? Didn't you think I'd be able to trace it back to you?"

The restaurant owner trembled.

"I'm telling you, John, I got no idea what you're talkin' about. I didn't tell Jenkins when you were collecting from your houses. How would I know that? I didn't even know you were in the crack business."

Frank took turns looking first at John, and then at Mike, then back at the TV screen, where the image of Samuel Jenkins Junior's now lifeless body sat, slumped over in the chair, his blank eyes staring a message into Frank's brain.

Be very convincing.

The gangsters in the room looked at each other, then back at Frank, prompting him to continue.

"When your butler came to see me at my restaurant, I didn't know he was involved in some stupid scheme."

John Salvatore walked over to the desperate man, who was failing miserably in his attempt to convince anyone of his innocence. The veins in his huge neck began doing their own little dance of death.

"YOU STILL THINK I'M FUCKIN' AROUND? I'M GONNA BLOW YOUR FUCKING HEAD OFF! YOU TELLIN' ME MY

FUCKING BUTLER WAS THE MASTERMIND BEHIND THIS? IS THAT WHAT YOU'RE FUCKING TELLIN' ME?"

The crime boss cocked the chamber back and pointed the gun at Frank's head.

"But you're a different story."

The restaurant owner closed his eyes before he spoke.

"The only thing I know, John, is what your butler told me, which wasn't much. Something about you holdin' out on him and him makin' sure you got yours. He was drunk, John. He was just talkin' out his head."

The pizza man was hoping to keep talking long enough for him to think. He couldn't guess what was going on in the psychopath's head. So he kept on.

"What does your butler have on you that would lead you to kidnap and torture his son? What, did you try to beat it out of him before you turned to the drugs? It went too far and he OD'd, right?"

He motioned towards the TV.

"Looks like you didn't get all the information you wanted. He must have told you something about their plans. That's how you were able to find out what happened so quickly."

The crime boss glared at him.

"But he didn't tell you what you really wanted to know. He had no idea what you were talkin' about. You thought he was holdin' out on you, but he wasn't. His father didn't tell him shit. And now, you're stuck."

The crime lord looked at Frank for a minute before withdrawing his .45 automatic, and putting it in his pocket. He turned and looked at the others with a sly smile.

"You know what, Collazo? You were always a smart guy. Even when we were kids, you were smart. You never got into the family, never got your hands dirty. You never thought of joinin' up with me. I used to wonder why. But now, I know. You think you're smarter than me. You figured you were too smart to take orders from somebody like me."

He turned to the short, balding man.

"You know what? You got it figured right. Jenkins thought he could blackmail me into signing some property over to him. He was plannin' to retire back down south. The land once belonged to his great-grandfather. The old nigger bought his freedom, and then bought this land to plant for himself. The black bastard did all right for a while. Made some money growin' tobacco. After the old man died, Jenkins' grandfather thought he was untouchable, but the Klan wasn't havin' no nigger success stories. So they made him a 'generous offer'. The bank's had it ever since."

"You should've seen his face when I told him I was the new owner of the land. He was pissed off," the gangster laughed.

"I've never seen him get angry before and it was funny. That old nigger told me I wasn't going to get in the way of his dream. Can you believe that?"

The other underworld figures in the room laughed, picturing the sight of old man Jenkins standing up to John Salvatore. The crime boss looked at Frank with the coldness he'd seen before.

"I told him the only dream he was to fulfill was the one in which he stayed working for me until the day he died. Which is exactly what happened now that I think about it," he said as an afterthought. The men in the room laughed again as the gangster sat behind his desk.

"What I want to know is this: Why did you get involved in my business? You lettin' the past fuck with your head again?"

The short, balding man who knew John Salvatore before he became "Greektown Johnny" knew the answer to that question.

He looked the mob boss directly in the eye. Time to get real.

"I had no choice. It was the first time I could connect you."

"Connect me? Connect me with what?"

"Let me refresh your memory. Shortly after you moved here, my dad was murdered for not paying protection money to the locals."

The gangster looked at him surprised.

"Guess who I think killed him."

Before the gangster could reply, the cell phone in his pocket started singing. The mobster had it set to the tune of Sinatra's "My Way".

"Yeah," he answered. "What's up? . . . Oh yeah?"

He looked at Frank smiling, his mood changing instantly.

"We'll be right there."

CHAPTER NINE

Hank Littlejohn entered Jimmy D's bar shortly before last call. He was reaching his breaking point in his quest to stay calm and in control. The delivery of Jenks' finger to his apartment blew calm/control out the water. How did they find out so fast? That question rolled around in his head like an out of control bowling ball. Scanning the dark nightclub, he spotted his younger brother sitting at a table with a young lady.

"Damn, Nate," he begun as he walked over to the table, "You ain't gonna believe what happen . . . "

"Hey, man," his brother interrupted. "Don't you speak to old friends anymore?"

In his haste to broadcast the latest development, Hank overlooked who was sitting at the table with Nathan. He assumed it was some tackhead Nathan was trying to bone instead of being the one girl he could never get next to. And he's been tryin for years.

"Hey Tia, how you doin'?" he said with obvious interest. "What you been up to? You ain't been answering your pager. You still got it on?"

Tia Day sat at the table, listening to Hank Littlejohn go on about nothing as usual.

"I'm doin' fine, Hank," she replied. "Just hangin' out with your brother for a minute. Have you been calling me?" she inquired innocently.

"Always, baby, always."

She tuned out his conversation to notice a huge white man heading for the exit. He was an extremely large man, big enough to draw attention just by standing up. Something about the man was familiar to her, she thought as he continued to make his way towards the door. Not too many white dudes came into Jimmy D's to hang out and the few that did were tryin' to score. Giving him the once over, she decided that wasn't his profile.

"So, Hank," she said, refocusing on him. "What happened? You sounded pretty freaked out when you came in here." Nathan gave his brother the look that made him think twice before he replied. Hank looked at Tia stone-faced.

"There was a drive-by near Jenks' house. We need to check it out."

Nathan could tell his brother was lying, but also knew from the earlier conversation that something bad went down. They had to leave. Now. But first he wanted to be sure Tia wouldn't say anything to her sister about Kay Brown. I must love drama and bullshit he decided.

Nathan glanced over and saw Kay sitting at the bar, watching them. She gave him a wink, then headed for the front door.

Good move, he thought, as she moved past their table without a glance in their direction. Not that it didn't go unnoticed by Tia. She decided to throw one more question at Nathan.

"I guess the DJ wore your girl out."

He frowned before responding.

"I told you, we not kickin' it anymore."

Her "black woman's expression" told him she wasn't buying what he was sellin'.

"So, you gonna tell your sister or what?" Tia took a long sip of her Chivas Regal and smiled.

"I don't know. Maybe, maybe not, I haven't decided," she lied.

Nathan gave her a disgusted sigh. Fuck it. He had bigger things to worry about. As Kay stood at the entrance of the nightclub, worry reentered his mind faster than Marion Jones on a good day. She stood there with a "Cheshire cat" grin on her face that somehow was illuminated in the dark nightclub, holding something. Something shining as bright as her grin. His eyes grew large as he recognized the objects in her hand. His keys. His car keys.

"SHIT!" He stood quickly, his hands going through his pockets in a futile attempt to make his keys magically reappear.

He looked at Tia, who was frowning at him intently.

His mind raced. Damn! He was so preoccupied he wasn't even aware that she had picked his pocket. What else was he ignorant of?

He stood, stunned, watching as she went through the door, laughing. This was bullshit.

He knew he had to get to his keys before she did something crazy. She had a thing for taking things that didn't belong to her.

Once, "back in the day," she took his car to go hang at the mall with her girls without his knowledge. He was asleep so she didn't think he'd mind. He threatened to call the cops the next time she did some bullshit like that.

She didn't respond well to threats.

The next day, she gripped it to Belle Isle Park.

"I left something in the car," Nathan lied. "I'll be right back."

Before Tia could protest, Nathan was out the door.

"Hank," he called over his shoulder. "Get Tia a drink."

Tia watched him go out the door, chasing after Kay. It pissed her off, the attention he was paying her.

"Did you see the way he ran after her?" she blurted.

"Who?" said Hank, turning back around in his chair.

She gave him another "B.W.E." She knew he wasn't this stupid.

"You know who, man. Kay Brown."

His round eyes grew large.

"Kay Brown was in here? Where?"

She looked at Hank, surprised.

"Well, well," she said dryly. "It looks like that bitch is Miss Popularity tonight. Everybody wants some."

Hank was in no mood for any games. He didn't have time for that.

"WHERE WAS SHE?" he said, grabbing her arm.

"MAN, YOU BETTER LET GO OF MY ARM!" her voice was rising.

"I DON'T PLAY THAT BULLSHIT!"

Some of the remaining patrons in the bar looked over at the table where the arguing couple sat. Two small-timers, known as Marvin and Sam, were watching especially hard. They were friends of Tia's, who wouldn't hesitate to kick some ass, if necessary. They were watching, waiting for the signal. From past experience, they knew she could take care of herself, so they stayed relaxed but alert. Just last week, a smooth operator tried to steal a squeeze on her well-formed ass. A beer bottle across his head guaranteed no repeat performances.

Hank saw how calm she was, which surprised him, considering how hard he was holding her. Then he remembered something Nathan told him about his girlfriend's sister.

That she was crazy.

That not too many brothers fucked with her. Drama had a way of following her around. Then he noticed how she seemed to be gripping her glass in a way that suggested hand-to-hand combat. He released her arm.

"My mistake," he said calmly. "I'm just trippin' on some shit that went down earlier."

"That's all right," she replied. "No harm done. Just don't do it again. When I want a roughneck, I'll let you know."

She was a tough girl. And getting sexier by the minute.

"So where's that drink?"

"Coming right up."

He signaled to the bar, getting "Jo DD's" attention, who gave him a slight nod.

"It'll be here in a minute. So tell me about Kay Brown."

Tia looked at Hank with a smirk while a curvaceous waitress set her drink down on the table, shot Hank a mean look for his weak-ass tip, then walked away.

"What do you want to know? She came in. She blew the DJ. She left. Same old shit."

Tia could be very blunt when she wanted.

"Did she come in with Nate?"

"Hell, yeah! But he's tryin' to play like she didn't."

She put the drink to her full lips and sipped. It was strong, just the way she liked it.

"She didn't spend too much time with him, though. She sat with some old dudes for a minute, probably hustlin' 'em for some cash or something, if I know that bitch. Then she hooked up with 'Heat.'"

She had a look of sniffing sour milk on her face.

"I told you what that was about."

"She blew the DJ? Right here?"

"No, Hank," she nodded. "At the DJ's booth. While the strobe lights were on. They think they wasn't seen, but I seen 'em."

"Well, there you go. No way's Nate gonna sit there while his woman's goin' down . . . "

"Hey, I didn't say she was his woman. I said they came in together. Probably was goin' bangin' somewhere before runnin' in to me. Bein' his woman is my sister's stupid-ass job."

She took another sip of her drink, this one longer. She shivered slightly, feeling its effects.

"She don't never listen to me about you street niggas."

As Hank watched her drink the liquor like pop, he realized that she was headed for "blew-out city." She started leaning forward slowly, suggesting the possibility of passing out face first into the table.

That wouldn't be sexy.

"You talk to your sister tonight? How's Jeri doin'?"

Tia considered his questions for a moment before deciding to ignore them.

"Where's Nathan?" she asked no one in particular, although Hank was still sitting at the table.

"Finish your drink," he said tersely. "Then we'll go find out."

*   *   *

When Nathan Littlejohn walked out of the bar, he expected to see Kay Brown by the entrance.

She wasn't there.

After all these years, he couldn't believe she was still pulling crap like this. It pissed him off that she was always playing games. Didn't she know tonight wasn't the night for this bullshit? He looked up and down the street to where his car was parked, then up the other way. Nothing.

If he had come out two seconds earlier, he would have seen her crouch down behind a minivan parked across from his car.

The two men in the dark sedan recognized her as the woman who walked into Jimmy D's with Nathan. The smaller of the two psychos enjoyed the story his hulking partner told him about the goings-on inside the bar, especially the sexual escapades performed by Littlejohn's "whore" girlfriend.

Vito informed his partner of the call he made to their boss. Nothing to do now but wait for instructions. While the huge killer was in the bar watching their prey, the little man was checking out the contents of Nathan's vehicle. Nothing of interest to them, just a 9 mm Beretta and half an ounce of marijuana. He grabbed the gun but had no use for the weed, since he considered drug use beneath him. He had just finished the Mustang shortly before the red Porsche pulled up. After they finished their job, the club would be waitin' for them. The sight of Nathan Littlejohn stepping out of the bar ended any more conversation for now.

Silence before work is crucial. The two men were thugs, killers, and psychopaths. But they were also professionals. Goose bumps went over Vito's olive-colored skin as he realized killing time was near.

"Where the hell did she go?" Nathan said aloud as the two streetwalkers from earlier strolled by slowly, looking him up and down. He knew what they wanted, but he wasn't interested.

"Excuse me, ladies," he said graciously, "but you didn't happen to see a woman running out of here a few minutes ago, did you? She's tall, about six feet, dark skin, real pretty."

"Yeah, we seen her," one of the whores said. "She came runnin' out like she was high, gigglin' and shit. See that minivan over there? You can't see her from here but that's where she was a minute ago."

"What do we get for the info, bro?" the other one piped in.

Nathan reached into his pocket and pulled out a twenty-dollar bill. He tore it in half, giving each woman one.

"Thanks, appreciate it."

The women looked at each other, then back at Nathan, who was gone, running down the street.

"Shit. That was an easy twenty."

"Hell, yeah!"

The two women walked off, proud of the fact that they got some money without having to get on their backs or knees. Their pimp, a frequent barfly at Jimmy's, was parked a few cars down, checking out the scene. He'd make sure their pride was short-lived.

Nathan approached the minivan cautiously, expecting Kay to jump out any second.

Another one of her fuckin' games, he thought angrily as he looked around the van, finding no one. She loved playin' games.

The killers watched from their car as Kay Brown crept along the sides of parked cars down Woodward. She went between the cars, keeping low, just out of Nathan's sight.

"COME ON, GIRL," Nathan shouted. "I AIN'T GOT TIME FOR THIS BULLSHIT."

"What do ya think?" the small gangster asked his brutish partner. "A lovers' spat or what?"

The huge gangster smiled, keeping his eyes on Kay. Something about her. The physical similarities between her and his girl intrigued him. But he still couldn't see her face.

"That broad is hot," Marcello announced to his partner, never losing sight of the ebony beauty. "She reminds me of somebody, maybe an actress or ... "

The little gangster was annoyed by his partner's newfound appreciation of black women, and let him know it. "Maybe she's one of those sluts from the club, eh?"

His partner looked at him, expressionless, before answering.

"Not all black women are sluts, Vito."

"Right," he said sarcastically.

"You know, you can really be an asshole sometimes."

The psycho flashed his immaculate dentistry.

"Part of my charm."

As the two killers disagreed on the various attributes that black women possess, the driver of the red Porsche observed the scene on the street in front of Jimmy's. A few moments earlier, she had decided to change her location from directly across Jimmy D's. Not a moment too soon. She didn't want to be seen. Not yet.

Jeri Day drove her car around the corner and turned into a driveway. From this spot, she could still see the front of the bar without being on display herself. She had barely parked when Kay Brown came running out. The sight of her laughing and giggling was enough to convince her that her sister might be right. *No way was this coincidence*, she thought as Nathan Littlejohn appeared next. What the fuck is Nathan doin' talking to those prostitutes? They must know that slut, Kay, since they're sluts themselves. Tia watched as the streetwalkers pointed over to where Kay was creeping. What are they up to?

With her attention focused on Nathan and Kay, she paid no interest in the dark sedan coming slowly up the street.

It stopped in front of the bar and then pulled into the parking spot where she had been previously.

As she watched Nathan run towards where Kay was, rage started building up inside of her again.

"I'm gonna kill that bastard," she announced to no one in particular.

That statement also ran through the mind of Detroit's number one gangster, as he lit a cigar and watched the scene unfold in front of him.

CHAPTER TEN

The sounds of slow music and loud Arsenio Hall – type barking came filtering up through the air vents of the small office. Frank Collazo figured that past-her-prime porn star, Vivica Foxxx, the latest headliner, had just stepped onto the stage of Pussycat's. He wished it was that hot, black actress who was in that space invasion blockbuster a few years back. He knew better than that, though. "Greektown Johnny" Salvatore operated a triple-x-rated house and he wasn't about to import some Hollywood talent to Detroit, particularly someone as high-class as that actress. But he could dream. Hearing the sounds of wolf whistles and clapping made him think of when he was a young man interested in overt sexual behavior. He often had a good time in the company of prostitutes. That was the only type of women he'd been with since his wife died of a heart attack a decade ago. Since then, he'd sunk himself into his business, with a few bouts with alcohol on the side.

"You know, it's funny," he began. "I haven't been in a relationship in over ten years, but right now I can't get getting laid out of my mind. You know what I mean?"

The other man in the room looked at him with a look of contempt on his face. He turned his glass of scotch up, then poured himself a refill, never putting the .45 caliber automatic he had trained on Frank Collazo's heart down.

"You think it was easy going without pussy for damn near thirty years? Look at me. You see any females hangin' on my shoulder?"

That was tragic, yet Frank almost laughed aloud.

Mike Garbarini was pissed off at the hand life dealt him. He was ready to make up for lost years and he wanted to start tonight. He felt Frank Collazo had the answers he was looking for. And he wanted answers more than he wanted pussy.

"So tell me somethin', Frank," he started, "When did you decide to fuck me? Did the cops say somethin' to ya to make you go punk? Or did you just say 'fuck it' and go on with your soon-to-be-short-ass life?"

The tension in the room suffocated Frank. He couldn't figure why Mike blamed him for his jail time, but he knew he'd better sing the right song.

"Man, I'm tellin' you," Frank pleaded. "I don't know what you think or why you think it, but I didn't fuck you. I went to the cops. I told them the deal. They told me don't worry about it. Everything was under control. They said they was keepin' you in protected custody till the trial. What did I know? Next thing I knew, they said you admitted to shootin' your old man."

He kept his eyes on the .45 automatic, waiting for Mike to react. The silence meant he could continue.

"I didn't believe it. I knew how you felt about guns. I knew you wouldn't use a gun to kill somebody. Shit, you wouldn't even shoot a rat. Then . . . "

He stopped, unsure of where to go from that point. He knew he had to be convincing.

Mike looked down on him, his face revealing a look foreign to Frank. Only if you've spent a long time incarcerated would you be able to recognize that look.

"Then what?" the ex-con demanded. "Don't stop now. You've got my undivided attention."

Frank looked at the godfather's desk, where the bottle of liquor still sat.

"Can I have a drink, Mike?"

The gunman looked over at the bottle, then shrugged his shoulders.

"Sure, I don't care," he said, motioning Frank over to the desk with the wave of his gun. "Don't fuck with me though. I didn't use it then, but I'll put a hole in your ass now."

The nervous restaurant owner walked slowly, deliberately, over to the desk. He sat on top as he poured the bottle.

"A couple of days after your old man died, I went back to the alley. I needed somewhere to think things over. Everybody was talkin' about how your old man use to beat the shit out of you for nothin. They said he deserved what he got. They said you would get off. The thing I didn't figure was him gettin' it with a gun."

The sweating, portly man turned his drink up before fixing another, which he drank just as fast.

"That's it?" Mike asked. "That's all you got?"

After a wipe of his sweaty brow, the nervous man continued.

"I thought about the beating you took and what you said about killing him. I said to myself, if I knew I was going to get another ass-kicking and I had access to a gun, would I get it? And would I use it?"

Mike stared at Frank for a few minutes, letting the words sink in to his mind. He knew deep down there was nothing Frank could have done, but the anger told him Frank was the one who talked him into going to the cops. He gave up his life on Frank's advice, while Frank got rich selling pizzas.

"After my old man busted me and Johnny smokin', he dragged me back to my place and beat the crap out of me. He threw me into the hall closet and the next thing I knew, I found the hammer. When he came at me, I clubbed him. I thought I knocked him out cold. I knew when he woke up, he was gonna come for me. So I broke the hell out."

Mike walked over to the desk and handed Frank his empty glass. With the gun still pointed at Frank's chest, he motioned for him to pour him a drink. Frank did so slowly, looking at Mike's face. He handed him the drink without a word. He knew Mike had thirty years' worth of talking to do.

"You know, before I came to see you, I went to the alley myself. I swore that sonofabitch wasn't gonna beat me anymore. I looked around to see if anybody was watchin'. When I knew it was cool, I went over to the spot where Johnny kept that piece." Frank watched the anger slowly fade from Mike's face. He was in a daze, as if he were telling the story for the millionth time.

"I held the gun in my hand," he continued in the same monotone.

"I felt the cold steel, and for the first time, I knew what my old man meant. With that gun in my hands, I knew nobody could fuck with me. So I put the gun in my pocket and I started for home. I would be ready the next time that bastard put his hands on me . . . "

His voice trailed off as if he were lost in the thoughts of thirty years ago, which he was.

"First, I decided to go by Johnny's place. I figured he'd go with me back to my joint, just in case my old man was ready to give some more, ya know? He told me when we was busted that if I needed some help, he'd be there. My old man looked at him and told him if he came by our place, he'd kick his ass, just like he did mine."

Mike turned his drink up and sat the empty glass on the desk. Frank poured him another.

"I stopped by his place, and he wasn't there. That's when I came to see you. You know the rest."

Frank looked at Mike and it felt like the old days for a moment.

"So you didn't shoot him then."

Mike looked at him with the anger returning quickly to his face. With that, he knocked Frank's drink over onto the old rug.

"Fuck you!"

Frank looked at him, carefully choosing his words.

"I'm not tryin' to bullshit you, Mike. I'm tellin' you what I know. The last thing I heard was the cops had you and the murder weapon and you confessed. I swear." The ex-con looked at his former childhood friend and realized he was speaking, what he believed to be the truth. Then he spoke quietly.

"I knew you was going to tell me what I should do. I always looked up to you and I knew you wouldn't steer me wrong. That's why I listened to you and went to the cops in the first place. I didn't shoot him. But if I did, I wouldn't be stupid enough to go to the cops with a gun on me."

Frank looked at him and asked the million-dollar question.

"So what did you do with it?"

Mike looked at him for a moment before answering.

"I gave it to Little Tony. I saw him when I was leavin' Johnny's. He told me he'd take care of it."

Frank's mind started racing with this new information.

"Tony never said anything about havin' the gun."

"Johnny came up to see me, right after I got sent up. He said Tony's family moved away. Someplace out west, I think."

Frank's face lit up.

"He said that?"

"What?" Mike inquired. Frank motioned to his glass on the old carpet. With the wave of the gun, Mike gave him permission to retrieve his glass. He reached over and picked it up, wiping it clean with his shirt before filling it up again.

"Tony's family didn't move away. He ran away. Disappeared. They were asking us for weeks what happened to him. I didn't know. Nobody knew. We looked up and one day he was just gone. I haven't seen him since."

He paused for a minute.

"He disappeared right after the cops sent you away. A couple days after you left, he was gone."

The two men were quiet for a few minutes. Both were in deep thought about things they haven't thought about in years.

How much of what they heard tonight was true, they both wondered. After thirty years, they both felt like they were on the verge of finding out the truth about that life-changing summer.

"Tell me, Frank," Mike said, breaking the silence. "What makes you think Johnny had something to do with your old man gettin' whacked?"

Frank looked at him for a minute before speaking.

"You gonna point that thing at me all night? I ain't goin' nowhere."

The ex-con thought for a second before putting his .45 automatic in his waist.

"Something the old butler told me," he began as Mike watched him take another sip of his drink.

"He told me that Johnny wouldn't let him quit 'cause he had to keep him around. He knew too many of Johnny's secrets. I pressed him for more but he wasn't sayin' shit else. One thing I do remember him sayin'. That every man had to honor his creator, and that's what he intended to do."

He paused for a moment before speaking again.

"He told me I need to honor my father. I asked him what he meant and he would say that it was in God's plan that I honor my father by seeking revenge on those responsible for his murder. I never talked to nobody about my fathers' murder. Nobody."

"So what's that mean?" Mike said. "He could have heard Johnny and some boys talkin' about old times. And that could be all bullshit."

Frank turned his drink up and finished it. He put the empty glass on the desk before looking up at Mike.

"Some of the east coast boys were in town a while back to see John. They were up at his place, gettin' drunk and shit. The butler said he heard Johnny braggin' about how his first murder was done. The police kept the details quiet 'cause they were thinkin' they could catch the killer when he slipped up. He never did, until now. Nobody, other than the cops, knew how my old man was killed. Them, and the killer."

Mike looked at his old friend and asked the question.

"So how was he killed?"

He looked Mike straight in the eye and Mike knew he spoke the truth.

"He was shot. Three times in the back and two in the head. Just like your dad."

CHAPTER ELEVEN

Detroit's number one mobster got out of the back seat of his car and stepped into the shadows of the damp, dark street. He stood alongside his car, relighting his Cuban cigar. He savored the taste as he watched the man, who earlier that day robbed five of his dope houses, look for the girl hiding behind some cars, just out of sight. Should he or shouldn't he? What the hell, he thought.

"HEY, BUDDY," he yelled at the man.

Nathan Littlejohn turned suddenly, wishing he hadn't left his 9 mm Beretta in the car.

The gangsters in the godfather's car and the two hitmen employed by the mobster in the other car had the same thought as they watched with confusion their boss. Was he crazy?

"YOU LOOKIN' FOR THAT CHICK THAT JUST CAME OUT OF THE BAR?" he shouted down the street.

Kay looked over at the old man, wondering what the fuck he was doing.

"YEAH," his young adversary responded. "YOU SEE WHERE SHE WENT?"

The old man pointed.

"SHE'S HIDING BEHIND THAT CAR OVER THERE."

He smiled and waved.

Kay looked at him, cursing. What the hell was he doing?

Nathan jumped out into the street before Kay had a chance to make a move.

"Hi, honey," she said meekly. "You ready to go?"

He walked swiftly over to her before she could stand up.

Holding his hand out, he waited in silence.

She reached up, holding his keys in her hand. He snatched the keys, then turned around, leaving her sitting on the street. *He was pissed*, she thought.

"Baby, you not upset, are you?" she said in her sweetest voice. "I was just havin' a little fun."

He turned and looked at her angrily.

"Was suckin' the DJ's dick while I watched fun too?"

Kay's facial expression went from carefree to anger in a heartbeat.

"What I do is my business," she shot back. "You ain't my man. You just somebody I fuck sometimes."

Nathan stared at her, wondering what he was doing with this lowlife bitch in the first place.

"You just mad it wasn't your dick I was on."

She walked up to him slowly, smiling seductively.

"Don't start actin' jealous now, honey. It's no problem when you jumpin' out my bed, rushin' to get home to your girl. Don't trip when I get my groove on with somebody else."

They stood looking at each other for a minute before Nathan broke the silence.

"I'm through with this foolin' around bullshit. I don't even know why I picked you up tonight."

She moved closer to him, rubbing her suddenly hard nipples against his chest.

"I know why."

He grabbed her by the shoulders and extended his arms, pushing her away.

"You don't understand what I'm sayin'. It's over. I should have told you weeks ago."

She's heard this speech before. Something was different this time.

"I can't keep fuckin' Jeri over like this. My relationship with her is too important to me."

Looking at his face, Kay knew their fun was over for now. When he was pissed like this, there was no talking to him.

"I was just fuckin' with you," she apologized. "You don't have to go there."

He looked at the front of the bar, where Hank and Tia stood.

They stepped out while he was talking to Kay. He knew he had to cut it short.

"Look, that's my girl's sister over there with my brother. We got some business to take care of. I can't finish this with you now, but I'll call you. I'm outty."

With that said, he turned and walked away. Kay stood there, her satisfaction of a few minutes ago gone.

"So you just gonna leave me here, huh? What am I supposed to do?"

He kept walking without turning around.

"Get a ride from the DJ. His way of thanking you for a good time."

"FUCK YOU, NATHAN!"

"Whatever," he replied over his shoulder as he walked over to Hank and Tia. They stood watching the "angry black couple show" that starred Nathan Littlejohn and Kay Brown. Here comes one of the co-stars now.

"Let's get the fuck out of here. Tia, you need a ride?"

She looked down the street at Kay Brown, still standing on her mark, spitting her lines out at the unseen television audience.

"Yeah, I'll go with you. I got a few questions for ya," she smiled, tilting her head towards the angry young woman.

"Fine, you ride with me. Hank, let's go to my spot."

Nathan's older brother didn't often disagree with his younger, streetwise sibling, but in this situation, Hank Littlejohn had the crucial knowledge. As Tia strained to listen, Hank quietly filled his brother in on the delivery of the five-hundred-dollar finger. Nathan's mind worked overtime, trying to figure all the possibilities that existed concerning "Greektown Johnny" Salvatore. As evident by this choice of message, he knew Johnny was capable of anything.

"Can you tell me how he found out so quickly?" Nathan implored. "I don't know. But I'd like to ask Kay Brown a . . . "

A slight shake of his brother's head told Hank to ice that line of conversation. He complied.

"I'll meet you at the King's Inn on Jefferson. Get a room and I'll be there in about twenty minutes."

The King's Inn was a cheap, old motel fifteen minutes from downtown. Hank spent many nights there with females, smoking weed, enjoying their company. They'd be safe there for a minute before making their next move.

"Tell the desk clerk you're my brother and to give you my usual room."

Tia looked at Hank with a look of disgust that said it all.

"I know what you're thinkin'," he said, returning her glare. "We can discuss us later."

"What us? There is no us. You talkin' crazy sh . . . "

That was as far as Tia got before Hank pulled her close and kissed her.

After watching the embrace for a couple of seconds, Nathan interrupted. "We don't need to be on the street. They ridin' around with some heavy shit to take us down with, you know what I'm sayin'? Ya'll can get busy later."

"You right," Hank agreed, releasing Tia from his arms. "Ride with Nate and we'll deal later."

Tia, caught off guard by Hank's sudden move, could only nod in stunned agreement.

The two men exchanged the universal grip of respect that black men give each other when arriving or departing. Then Hank walked towards his car.

The gangster watched with quiet pleasure as the three people on the street talked, he assumed, about what their next move would be. It intrigued him that a small timer would have the balls to even consider hitting one of his operations, let alone pulling it off. It was an excellent game plan, but it was doomed from the start. He thought about how easy it was to catch Samuel Jenkins Jr. You can't rely on junkies. They'll always bring you down.

Johnny watched the trio continue to make plans. The tall man's body language told the godfather he was the mastermind behind the heist. It was rare that the mobster was impressed with someone outside his own organization, but impressed he was with Nathan Littlejohn.

"I got it set up, boss," the small assassin said to the crime czar, interrupting his thoughts. "Everything's ready."

The man he talked to moments earlier, and the woman, walked down the street, towards the Mustang. As he continued to watch them, he pulled another of his expensive cigars. Lighting it, he thought about the day thirty years ago when he was busted with Mike Garbarini. Mike's dad threatened to beat his ass if he came by his place again. As he began blowin' smoke rings, an odd smile appeared on the gangster's face. If that bum could see him now, he'd be beggin' for a job.

"Anytime, boss," the little psychopath interrupted again.

"I'll tell you when I'm ready, Vito," the boss snapped.

The huge assassin, feeling his partner's discomfort, smiled.

"What the fuck happened to your shirt?" he said, pointing to the large stain on his shirt. "You look fucked up."

The small assassin turned around, facing the front.

"Nothin'. Marcello soaked me with a sausage, is all," he said, embarrassed.

"Jesus, you look terrible," the crime boss assured. He began to laugh. "I bet you shit in your pants, eh?"

Marcello Baldino smiled again.

"You goin' to the club, boss?" he said, changing the subject.

"No, not yet. I still got some unfinished business at the Pussycat," he answered. "Old business. Something I should've handled years ago. All right, Mr. Clean, get ready."

The little killer didn't find his new nickname to his liking.

Hank Littlejohn watched his brother and the fine woman he was with walk down the street. Looking at her ample behind move back and forth, he smiled, thinking about the kiss they just shared. He'd wanted to do that for years. Why he grabbed her then, he didn't know. But it felt good. *I gotta make a more serious effort to get with her. Maybe when things die down a bit,* he thought. Putting the rest of the joint he was smoking earlier in his mouth, he looked into his glovebox for a lighter. Not there. Frustrated, he began looking in between the seats and on the floor.

"Ah," he said, spotting the 99-cent disposable, partly hidden under a napkin on the floor. He reached across the seat to retrieve the flame.

The gangsters in the car parked down the street from Hank Littlejohn were waiting. It was moments like these that the mob boss enjoyed, the anticipation, the feeling that he was in total control. Being a control freak with a huge ego that needed constant feeding, it was no surprise that he enjoyed turning the knife once he had it in his victim's back.

"Hand me those binoculars, Marcello," John ordered. The boss always demanded that his boys carry a pair with them on jobs. He liked to see the results up close and personal. Next to watching tapes of his executions, this was his best entertainment.

The mobster watched as the image of a man enjoying a smoke came into view. He watched the man inhale the smoke from the tiny joint and wondered how it tasted.

"Hey," he said, startling the professional killers in the front seat. "Either of you two smoked marijuana?"

Surprised by the question, they looked at each other for a second, unsure of how to answer.

"Not me, boss," Vito answered first. "I think that shit damages the brain. Makes ya forget everything."

"That's what I was told, anyway," he added a second later.

"What about you, Bear?" the godfather inquired. "I know you like to try new shit."

"Well," he began. "Sometimes I run across some at the clubs I go to. They always lookin' to sell nickel or dimes to the dance crowd."

"Who is they?"

"Small timers. Dudes that get just enough to satisfy the locals."

He turned and looked at his boss.

"Anything over a pound, we get a piece of."

Detroit's number one criminal was satisfied with the answers.

"Good. Just 'cause it's nickel-and-dime shit don't mean we can't make some serious money off of it."

He looked into his spyglasses again. It was time.

"All right, Vito. Now."

The tiny assassin held a small remote control box on his lap. It looked like one of those universal remotes that you can get from any Radio Shack or Best Buy to control your TV, VCR, or cable box. The one he held was specifically designed to meet their own needs. The small hitman held up the remote and pointed it towards a car where, less than an hour ago, he had placed three explosive caps. His source at the army base swore they would do the job. They were tested in the Gulf War and passed with flying colors. The mobsters would soon find out. He pushed the button.

In a microsecond, all the plans and all the dreams Hank Littlejohn had for his life after the heist were over. A sudden, powerful blast of fire woke the night up, breaking the windows of ten cars, several apartments, and the twenty-four-hour convenience store on the corner. Hank Littlejohn died instantly, his charred and mangled body thrown from the twisted, burning hunk of metal that use to be his car. His lifeless form landed on the hood of a brand-new BMW parked fifty feet down the street, causing the proud owner and his date to stop making out and become horrified.

Reaction came quickly from all sections of the neighborhood. People came running out of the apartment building, the bar, and the row of rundown, two-family flats down the street. Kids waking up from their sleep began pleading with their parents to let them look out the window to see what happened. Dogs began howling and barking as the sound of sirens began to fill the air. Police and fire officials had to end their mundane midnight-shift routines while all the activity that accompanies a huge accident began. Amidst the confusion and panic, two people raced towards the car.

Nathan Littlejohn couldn't believe that the burned, unrecognizable body that was on the BMW was his brother. He stood there in shock. His eyes watered as he realized the person he counted on most in this world was dead. And he knew why.

"Nathan. Nathan, come on. We got to get out of here".

A voice he could barely hear was pleading with him to leave his brother. "NO, NO!" he cried pulling away from Tia's grip. "GET THE FUCK AWAY FROM ME! I AIN'T GOIN' NOWHERE!"

Tia Day knew that Nathan was in shock. He wasn't thinking clearly. She had to make him understand that they had to leave. There was nothing he could do for his brother now. "Nathan," she said, trying to stay calm. "You think whoever got to Hank is going to forget you?"

She hesitated, hoping the words were getting through to him. He looked at her, slowly understanding the situation.

"We got to get out of here. Now."

He looked at the burned corpse for a few seconds before he realized a crowd had gathered around them, encircling them. He looked around, hoping to see something, anything, that could give him some answers. What he saw was the flashing lights of police. He knew he couldn't be here for their arrival. He turned and looked at his brother for the last time.

"I'm gonna get those muthafuckas," his shaky voice trembled. "Believe that."

The man most responsible for the crime sat in the car parked down the street, still observing the events through his binoculars. *There shouldn't be any doubt about who was behind this*, the godfather thought. He looked at the pain and hurt in the face of Nathan Littlejohn. He entered the big time when he crossed "Greektown Johnny" Salvatore. And now, he was paying the price.

"You'll soon be next, my friend."

As if waiting for just the right moment, the cellular phone in Johnny's pocket began singing "My Way." He smiled in anticipation of who it might be.

"Yes," he answered. "I thought I would be hearing from you . . . yes, everything's going fine . . . were you worried that he would get hurt? . . . I didn't think so. Where is he going now? . . . Because I'm paying you to know. . . you think I keep you around just for your looks? If you can't help me, you're no good to me . . . that's what I thought . . . Fine. When you have something, call me."

He put the phone down and spoke to the mobsters in the front seat of the car for the first time since the explosion.

"You guys gonna sit here all night? I got business back at the club."

He stepped out of the car as two police cars flew past. The gangster smiled, thinking of how inept they were. Before he walked across the street to his waiting sedan, he tapped the drivers' window. The large hitman rolled it down to receive instructions.

"Follow him. I want to know every move he makes. I want to have my money in my hands before the sun comes up, you hear me?"

The huge man nodded. He was a professional and he knew what his boss expected. He'd never lost a job before and he knew he wasn't about to start now.

"One more thing."

The city's number one criminal looked at the young couple frantically run over to the Mustang GT. His eyes focused on the brown-skinned beauty standing next to the car as the driver checked under the hood for any signs of tampering. *What a waste*, he thought. He turned back to the killer.

"No witnesses."

The mob boss turned and looked at the scene once more before returning to his car. Firemen were successfully extinguishing the fire while the police were not so lucky in their efforts to control the crowd. While they were busy at the accident site, looters were busy at the convenience store. Spotting the scene at the store, the crime boss shook his head.

"That's the trouble with them people," he said to his henchmen. "They just don't respect the law."

He sat in the car and prepared another cigar.

"Let's go. I got more fish to fry."

Jeri Day sat stunned, watching the chain of events unfold in front of her. She felt bad about Hank. She always got along with him and knew he wished nothing but good things for her and Nathan. And now, he was dead. Involved in one of his brother's get-rich-quick schemes. Nathan promised her the world when she saw him last. What did they do to deserve this?

She watched as her sister tried to comfort Nathan, only to have him pull away in anger. And guilt. *I should be with him*, she thought. Her anger melted away with the explosion as she watched her man grieving. Then she spotted something unusual.

While the street was in chaos, with people rushing and screaming, one person remained calm and composed. Walking down the street at a deliberate pace away from the scene was Kay Brown. She was talking on her cell phone, never once turning back to look at the wreckage. *She was probably spreading the news about Hank already,* Jeri thought. After a moment of watching Kay, her attention went back to the Mustang GT. She watched as Nathan and her sister checked out the car. Holding her breath, she let out a sigh of relief as it started without incident. As the Mustang GT took off down Woodward, tires smoking, she hoped he wouldn't do anything crazy. Hopefully, Tia would calm him down. Right now, she needed some questions answered. As Jeri started to get out of her car, the woman she resumed to watch stopped at the corner and pointed to a brand-new Lexus. The familiar beep-beep of the horn and the quick flash of the lights meant the alarm was now deactivated. *When did Kay Brown get a new Lexus?* Tia wondered as she watched her enter the luxury car. She pulled out slowly, making sure she had plenty of room to maneuver.

The new sports car pulled out on Woodward, heading in the opposite direction Nathan went a few minutes earlier, towards downtown. Jeri started the 924 Porsche and pulled out of the driveway she'd been parked in for the last half an hour. As she turned her car onto Woodward, she looked into the rearview mirror to see the EMS technicians removing what was left of Hank Littlejohn. They put the covered remains on a stretcher, then into the back of the ambulance. Destination: The morgue. As she headed towards downtown, a couple of car lengths behind the Lexus, she caught images of a half-dressed man and woman standing near the BMW, attempting to answer the police's questions. The images grew smaller and smaller as she raced into the early morning.

CHAPTER TWELVE

Mike Garbarini stood silently, letting the words Frank Collazo told him digest.

"That don't mean nothin'," the ex-convict said. "That sounds like a standard hit to me."

"I'm tellin' you, Mike. Three to the back, two to the head. That's Johnny's MO for years. Don't you want the truth?"

"That's all I've been thinkin' about for twenty-seven years."

"Then we got to go. There's nothin' I can do here."

His childhood friend looked at the restaurant owner with a weary eye. He would say anything at this point to save his life.

"So you got proof?"

Frank looked at him for a moment before answering.

"Not here. Not on me."

"Yeah, right. I can see John's face now when I tell him, forget the orders, Frank and me are gonna hang out. You don't mind, do ya? We'll be back."

"So you are in his pocket."

They sat quietly for a minute until the silence was broken by the sound of . . .

RING. RING. RING.

On the fourth, Mike answered. Frank knew who was on the line.

"Hello? Yeah, John . . . yeah, we been catchin' up . . . some of the shit he's tellin' me . . . yeah, unreal. How's it goin' with you? Oh yeah, that should make the morning news, maybe the papers . . . yeah . . . uh-huh . . . that's good . . . yeah . . . All right . . . I got things covered here . . . "

He looked at the nervous pizza man.

"Yeah . . . trust me."

Mike put the phone down and walked over to the lone window in the room. He looked out at the street below. It was quiet now.

"What happened?" Frank asked. "What should make the papers?"

For a brief moment, he thought about making a break for the door. Something inside him made him stay where he was. The ex-con turned and faced him, his hand on the butt of his .45 automatic.

"John caught up to one of your buddies. You know, one of your partners in crime. He won't be rippin' off nothin' no more."

The restaurateur began sweating.

"Yeah, he said it was something out of the Gulf War. You'll read about it in the papers. Maybe."

Frank Collazo knew he didn't have much time. If he was gonna make a move, it had to be soon.

"What's it gonna be, Mike? You wanna know the truth?"

Mike Garbarini walked over to where Frank was standing and looked at him, silent. When he spoke, he left no doubt about his intentions.

"All right," he said calmly. "We'll play it your way. Whoever stood by while I was sent up is gonna pay big time. It plays out your way, I'll take care of things. It's my business now. But if you're wrong and John's right . . . "

He drew his gun, pointing it at Frank's chest.

"Let's just say you better be real convincing. If Johnny's behind my frame-up, he's gonna wish I had another thirty years to do. Either way, somebody's gonna pay."

The gunman pointed towards the door, then put the gun inside his pocket.

"Let's go."

The two men left the room above the triple-x-rated palace and went downstairs. The club was now empty, except for a few stragglers. After whispering something in the hulking brute Gino's ear, Mike directed Frank to the alley, where his car was waiting.

"Get in," Mike ordered. "You drive."

Frank Collazo got behind the wheel of Mike's 88 Buick and pointed it into the direction of downtown.

"You hungry, Mike?" Frank asked.

"Yeah, I'm hungry. I ain't ate in a few hours."

He looked at all the changes in the area since he's been away. It made him realize how much he'd missed.

"Man, everything's new. I remember that used to be the Arcadia skating rink," he said, pointing to the mini-mall. "You couldn't fuck around in there if you couldn't skate."

"I remember," the driver replied.

Mike reached over and clicked on the radio. It was on the jazz station, as usual. Mike always did love jazz, Frank thought. He glanced over at the passenger who was nodding his head slowly with the Coltrane tune that filled the car.

"Where we goin', Frank?"

"To my place at the Ren Cen. I got a restaurant there."

The Renaissance Center was a Motor City success story.

After the scars of the riots in the late 'sixties healed, Detroit was in need of something to pave the way for a new era. It was the Ren Cen. It housed hotels and restaurants, offices and nightclubs. It was the jewel of Detroit, and Frank Collazo felt proud to have his headquarters there.

"You doin' real good, eh, Frank?" his old friend inquired.

"I can't complain. Took a lot of work, though."

They continued the rest of the trip in silence, each man lost in thought. They soon arrived at the downtown complex.

Turning right off Jefferson Avenue, they entered the building's underground parking lot facility.

"I'm on the thirty-third floor," Frank said as he maneuvered the car into a parking space. "Do you want to stop at the restaurant and grab a pizza? It's on the ground floor."

"Sure. Why not?"

They crossed the empty garage to the elevators. As they moved across the quiet structure, the only sound heard was their footsteps. Frank decided to break the silence.

"Mike," he began. "I know I let you down. I know I should've come see you . . . "

"You goddamn right you should've come see me," Mike interrupted. "But you ready to kill me over that? What did I do to deserve this?" Mike looked at his former friend.

"Let's wait for the elevator," he said, looking up at the up and down arrows.

"Look, there's no reason for me to lie to you. What has Johnny been telling you all these years? That I was responsible? That I could have made a difference? I didn't know nuthin. All I knew was what you told me."

The elevator doors opened, the solitude of the small chamber awaiting. They walked inside, where Frank pushed the close button. As he reached for the ground floor button, Mike grabbed his arm, preventing him from pushing the button.

"I changed my mind about the pizza," he explained.

As the elevator rose quickly through the tall glass structure, the ex-convict began to tell his old partner in crime what was told to him.

"Johnny was comin' to see me every month. I'd asked him where the fellas were and he'd laugh. Said you guys didn't have the time to come check me out. Ya'll was too busy."

He glared, reliving the memory.

"Told me about Tony's family movin' away so I wasn't too pissed at him. They moved pretty far away so . . . "

"I told you what happened to Tony . . . "

"Shut up. Don't interrupt," Mike said. "So, like I was sayin', he said Jimmy was killed in a car crash, and you . . . "

He stared at Frank's eyes like he did back at the strip joint.

"You was gettin' big time with your old man's pizza joints. Makin' serious money. Livin' the life. But that's okay. You didn't owe me nothin'. I was just your best friend, that's all."

Frank looked at the numbers on the wall, hoping for number 33. It was only on 10.

"He told me somethin' I couldn't believe."

"What did he tell you?"

"Wait till we get to your office. Then you can show me your proof."

A couple of seconds later, they were on the floor, standing outside Frank's main headquarters. After unlocking the door with the keyless entry system, they moved inside.

Frank hit the light switch on the wall to reveal a magnificent view of downtown Detroit. The office was spectacular with plush carpeting, soft leather furniture, the standard wet bar, and the latest state-of-the-art computer system. On the far wall, he had seven TV monitors, covering all of his restaurant. Frank walked over to his desk, where he pushed a button on a huge remote control. The TV screens came to life, displaying seven different images. Mike stood in the middle of the room, looking everything over. After glancing at the TV monitors for a second, he made his way over to the bar.

"Nice office. I assume those images are your other restaurants. Kinda dark in there."

"It's four in the morning. Ain't nobody there at four A.M."

"So, you got that same electronic shit that Johnny's got at your Woodward restaurant. How'd he install cameras in there without you knowin'?"

"When his boys were installin' the cable, I bet. You know he's got a piece of that company too."

As Mike watched him closely, Frank crossed the plush office over to his bar, where Mike was sitting. He stepped behind the bar and fixed a scotch. He handed the drink to Mike before fixing one for himself.

"So," he began. "What was it that you couldn't believe?"

Mike turned his drink up before putting the empty glass on the bar.

"Johnny told me how after I got sent up, you were sayin' how you wouldn't have ever put up with the shit I did. That you couldn't wait to take over for your old man. He said you wanted a bigger slice of the pie, but your old man had other ideas. He wanted you to go to school, maybe college, but you weren't down with that. You wanted your shit now and he was in your way."

Frank finished his drink, and then proceeded to pour another round for himself and his guest.

"Go on."

The ex-con took another sip before he continued.

"Bottom line is when the word came down about your old man not payin his dues, the family was ready to cut a deal with him. You didn't know this but your father was already cleanin' money for them. He was ready to make the deal and retire to easy street. Next thing you know, your old man's dead."

"So where's the confusion?" the restaurateur asked. "They changed their mind about payin' him and ordered Johnny to take him out."

"Nope. Not how it happened. I checked. You can find out a lot of shit in prison."

Frank walked back over to his desk. He sat on the top and looked at Mike, as he continued with the story.

"They didn't give the word," he explained. "It would have been bad for business. It wasn't always their style to force owners to sell against their will. Their first choice was to offer so much money, you'd be a fool to turn 'em down. You think it's good business to murder? Customers don't return to a place where they fear for their lives."

"So what does that mean?" he asked, not really wanting to hear the answer.

"It means they think somebody inside the family had a hit out on him. Talk was, your old man had a big mouth and had to be silenced. You can't draw attention to yourself in this business and your old man loved people to know he was connected. He had to go. Still . . . "

"Still . . . "

"Some of the boys think you had a hand in on it."

"That's crazy," Frank objected. "I was only 14. I wasn't ready to run no business. I loved my old man. I couldn't do something like that. But that's Johnny all over."

"Look," Mike began. "We could argue this all night. But we don't have all night. You got something that'll prove that Johnny set me up and killed your old man. So let's see it."

Frank rose from on top the desk and walked over to the bookcase, which was packed to the hilt with books. On the second shelf, he pulled three thick books towards him. When the books were ready to come out of the shelf, they seemed to stick in place. Suddenly, the whole bookcase slid away from the wall. Mike walked over to the bookcase as Frank reached behind it and pulled out an old book.

Frank blew the dust off of the book and walked back over to his desk, carrying the book carefully.

"What the hell is that?" Mike asked as he followed him back to the desk.

He laid the book on his desk carefully before sitting down.

"My Bible. I'm not a particularly religious man, but this is one of the few things my old man left for me. It's got an interesting letter in there that should open your eyes."

Just as he was about to hand Mike the letter, he pulled back.

"You know that if John finds this letter, I'm a dead man."

Mike shrugged his shoulders.

"What the hell, you might be a dead man anyway."

He handed Mike the letter.

As he read the letter, Frank explained the situation to Mike, trying to make him understand.

"You think Johnny killed him because of some land or because he wanted to retire? Bullshit. Jenkins had something Johnny wanted. Something that could prove who really killed your dad and mine."

Mike kept reading the letter as Frank watched intently, waiting for a reaction. He didn't have to wait long.

"Hey, man," Mike said excitedly, ""According to this, Jenkins knew what happened the night my old man bought it. He's got everything listed in just the way I said it happened. But this don't prove nuthin."

"Keep readin'. It substantiates your story. But the best part is that it suggests that he knew what happened to the gun you gave Little Tony. Check out the next page."

Mike turned over the letter and read the second page.

What he found was another letter, this one much more than he anticipated. It was a copy of a letter detailing a complex payment schedule. There were payments going back at least twenty-five years, the first one a couple of months after Mike went to prison, the last only a few weeks ago. All going to the same place: 21900 Swanson Ave., New York.

"So who's Johnny payin' off? What this got to do with the gun?"

"I did some checkin' myself. For the last twenty-seven years, 21900 Swanson Ave., New York, has been the home of our good friend, the formerly missing Tony Caramandini."

Mike's jaw dropped.

"Johnny told me he disappeared. Ran away."

"I know. He hadn't seen or heard from him."

The ex-convict thought about the implications the letter made. It seems Johnny's been lying to him for almost thirty years.

"How long have you known about this?" Mike asked.

"When Jenkins first approached me downstairs a couple of months ago. He knew what his boy and his friends were planning, so he figured he'd give them a little something extra. You know, just in case. For some reason, he trusted me. He told me to hold on to this package for him and he would pick it up from me soon. His boy was a crackhead and he couldn't trust him with it. When I heard he was missin', I decided to open it. I think he wanted me to have it all along."

Frank looked at the dusty Bible on his desk, caressing it slowly.

"He knew what he was talkin' about."

Mike looked at the letters again.

"So this connects Johnny and our fathers' murders. The old man tell you anything else?"

"He told me I needed to honor my father and avenge his death."

Mike looked at the letters again, then at Frank.

And the pizza man knew he believed.

CHAPTER
THIRTEEN

The two people in the Mustang GT were each lost deep in thought, letting the events of a few minutes ago sink in. It was one of those moments that you hope would never come, a time when you felt absolutely helpless and empty. And guilty.

Nathan Littlejohn was feeling all those emotions as he pushed the sports car to the limit. Going down Woodward at a high rate of speed was dangerous. There were many people out on the street, still looking for something to get into before calling it a night. Any of them could step into the street and in the way of the mourning driver. His vision, blinded by the hurt in his heart and mind, wasn't on the street in front of them.

"NATHAN, LOOK OUT!" Tia shouted.

A small car pulled out from the curb when the Mustang came roaring by. Before they knew what happened, the Mustang clipped the front quarter panel of the small European sports car, sending it back into the curb.

"Damn, Nathan. You better slow down before we get killed. I want to get home in one piece," Tia scolded.

Nathan looked at her, barely aware of the small collision they just had.

"Home? I ain't takin' you home. Not right now. I need you to come with me."

She looked at him like he was crazy.

"Ah, excuse me," she began. "You said you were taking me home. Where are we going?"

"We gonna run to the crib. I gotta pick up a few things."

Tia started to protest but thought better. Let him handle things for now.

Wait and see.

Nathan slowed the car down. He pulled into a closed gas station, next to a drive up pay phone. He then turned off the lights and turned the car off. They sat in silence for a second before Nate turned on the radio. The light from the street illuminated the car with a soft glow. For a minute, the soft jazz and soft lights made things seem surreal. The burnt smell in their clothes and noses was a reality check.

Nathan reached under his seat and pulled out a small baggie of marijuana. He put a small portion of the weed onto a tray. Rolling the bag up, he put it in his pocket and in the same motion, pulled a pack of rolling papers out. He proceeded to roll a joint as Tia watched. When he was done making the cigarette, he put the tray back in its place. Then he froze like a deer in oncoming traffic.

Fuck! FUCK, FUCK, FUCK!

Nathan reached further under his seat, only confirming what he suspected.

Sometime during their time together tonight, Kay Brown lifted his piece. He was sure of it. Why did she pick tonight to lift his shit?

THAT BITCH. ALWAYS PLAYIN' FUCKIN' GAMES!

That's what he felt like screaming. But screaming at the top of his lungs wasn't his style. He kept his thoughts to himself. Instead of trippin', he would stay cool. That's how he would play things for the moment.

Cool.

After taking a couple of hits off the joint, he passed it to Tia.

"This has been a fucked up night," Nathan said with exceeding coolness.

"Yes, it has," she agreed as she hit the illegal cigarette.

"I can't believe how fucked up things got. We was in and out in no time. Nobody seen our faces. How did they find out so quick?"

"How did who find out? Who did you guys rip off? I knew you

was still trouble. I been tellin' Jeri that but she won't listen. Maybe, she will now . . . "

"I'm gonna call her," Nathan said, suddenly cutting her off. "They might go to her place. She don't know shit, but they ain't gonna believe that. I gotta call her.

You got a quarter? I got no change."

Tia dug in to her pants and produced a quarter.

"Here," she said, handing the coin to him.

Trying to put the change into the coin slot was not easy for someone whose palms were sweaty, but he succeeded. One ring. Two. Three.

"No answer."

"Give it a few more rings," her sister said, trying to sound positive. In truth, she was starting to worry. Why hadn't Jeri paged her yet?

The phone rang for the fifth time before the answering machine came on.

When the familiar voice came on, he put the receiver down. Something wasn't right. He could feel it.

"Where the hell is she?" he turned and faced Tia.

"You told me you hadn't talked to her all night. You stickin' with that?"

"I told you I didn't. She's probably sleepin' hard, with the ringer turned down low," she lied. "She does that when she is tryin' to shut out the world."

Enough waiting. She started her questions coming with the quickness.

"So what're you gonna do? How long we gonna stay here? What do you need me for?"

Her questions were endless.

"How is my sister involved in this bullshit? Who did you try to rip off? What happened to Jenks? I heard Hank say somethin' about his finger or something."

"ALL RIGHT, ALL RIGHT! I'LL TELL YOU BUT YOU GOTTA CHILL ON THEM GODDAMN QUESTIONS!"

"ALL RIGHT!" she responded.

He put the half-smoked joint back in his mouth and lit it again. In between puffs, he told Tia the events of the previous day. They were suppose to lie low before taking separate flights to Las Vegas, where the money was to be sent by courier to be deposited in the accounts of the Motor City/Las Vegas Traveling Club of Detroit that Nathan opened three months ago.

After withdrawing the now clean money from the dummy business accounts, all they had to do was split the loot and go their separate ways. That was before everything blew up in their faces. His brother was dead. Jenks was dead. And now, he couldn't find Jeri.

"I was gonna swoop her up and we would be outty. Cash waitin' for us to do whatever we wanted. Now, that don't mean shit. What matter's is finding your sister. And gettin' the mothafuckas who killed my brother and my boy."

Tia looked at Nathan, really looked at him, for the first time since the explosion. He looked rough, tired. But you know what? He didn't look scared. Or shaken. He looked confident. He looked sure. He looked cool. Very cool. She knew at that moment that she could trust him. How much of what she knew could help?

"I guess I should tell you what I know."

She told him everything she knew from the time she saw him enter the bar with Kay. When she explained that Jeri should have met them there but didn't show up, the sweat that had been running off and on started flowing again.

"Shit, I knew something was wrong. We goin' by her crib now!"

He put the Mustang in drive, accelerating quickly. The quick move caught Tia off balance, causing her arm to hit the dashboard.

"SHIT!" she cried at the impact. She began rubbing her arm, where a bruise would be visible tomorrow.

"Sorry. I didn't mean . . . "

"That's all right," she said quietly. Tia looked at him, a puzzled expression on her face.

"What you thinking?" Nathan hesitated, then spoke slowly. "Those mothafuckas went to the crib and grabbed her, that's why we can't find her."

Tia's eyes began to water up as she thought about her sister ending up like Hank, a victim of some shit Nathan's gotten them into.

"Well, come on, we got to do something," she demanded.

"Slow down, girl. We gonna do something but we ain't gonna rush into nothing, youknowwhatimsayin'?

They drove in silence for a while, passing the joint between them, each lost deep in thought. Then she broke the ice.

"Nate, what made you think you could get away with rippin' off 'Greektown Johnny'?" He answered without hesitation.

"Not too many people knew that Jenks' dad was that muthafucka's butler. He gave us the info on when the money would be large. All we had to do was show up and collect. Now, everything's fucked."

Nathan slowed the car as he turned to look into Tia's eyes.

"I've got to find Jeri."

"You mean we have to find her." He looked at her, surprised.

"We, huh?"

"Uh huh."

"SHIT," he said, adjusting his rearview mirror.

"What?"

"We've got company. There's a set of headlights that's been on our ass since we left Jimmy's. I wasn't sure at first."

She turned around in her seat to see the lights a half block behind them.

"When I've slowed, they slow. When I speed up, they speed up."

Tia turned around in her seat, her eyes growing wide.

"They've kept their distance so far. Let's see what kind of a driver 'Greektown Johnny's' got. Hold on!"

With a slight smile on his face, Nathan punched the gas pedal of the muscle car, sending it furiously into the crisp morning air.

"Shit," said the driver of the assassin's car. "They seen us."

"Well, what the fuck you expect?" his small partner exclaimed. "You been on his ass so tough, it's a wonder why we ain't been made sooner."

"Fuck you, Vito," Marcello retorted. "I'm the best in the business and you know this."

"Just don't lose 'em now." The dark sedan accelerated behind the Mustang, desperately trying to maintain visual contact. That was easier said than done. If the gangsters knew the talent Nathan Littlejohn possessed behind the wheel of a car, they would've known that half a block was too great a distance to cover. After staying with the high-powered car for a couple of miles up Woodward Avenue, Marcello Baldino proved he was a better assassin than wheel man, as some superior driving by their adversary left the hoods unavoidably smashed to a tree. Thanks to the knowledge Nathan had of his neighborhood, he knew which turns to take hard and when to be easy. The gangster's reckless maneuvering thru Palmer Park proved they were ignorant of the sharp turns that awaited them.

Tia Day was growing more impressed with her sister's boyfriend by the minute. She had begun to have serious doubts about his ability to handle this situation, until she saw firsthand how calm and in control he was as they zoomed through the city with those hoodlums on their tail. When she wasn't closing her eyes in fear, she was peeking at the driver of the sports car she was riding in. *He almost seemed to enjoy the chase,* she thought, as they made one sharp turn after another, barely missing a row of parked cars once and some oncoming traffic down Hamilton, in the process. When the gangsters' car skidded into that tree in Palmer Park, she threw her arms around Nathan, letting out a joyous cry of relief, surprising her and him. They both felt in control for the first time since the explosion. Now, it was time to turn the tables. Nathan pulled the Mustang over to take a look at the wreckage that was the gangsters' car. He had to see who they were.

"What are you doing?" Tia exclaimed as he turned off the car.

"I've got to check this out." He unlocked the glovebox and pulled out yet another gun. A .38 special. Something his daddy told him once when he was about 14 that he never forgot. A gun can be a good thing to have or a bad thing to need. Treat it like you would a tire or a woman. Always have a spare.

"Stay here."

Nathan proceeded slowly towards the mangled wreck. The sound of steam escaping from the broken radiator filled the air. As he drew closer to the wreckage, Nathan could barely make out a low moaning sound. He raised his gun, pointing it at the car as he moved closer. Leaning into the driver's side, he could clearly see inside the destroyed vehicle. Not a pretty picture.

Whoever had been sitting in the passenger seat took the force of the impact the hardest. A thick limb of the tree came thru the windshield on impact, catching the man full force in the face. His nose, along with the $10,000 bridgework, was driven back into his brain, killing him instantly. "Little Vito's" days of fine clothes, fast women, and brutalizing victims were over.

The driver was still alive. He was pinned in as the steering wheel held him against the seat. For some reason, the airbag didn't inflate. His only visible injury appeared to be his right leg, which was bent in an unnatural position. Nathan leaned over to examine the driver closer. His face was familiar to Nathan. As he did, the large man coughed, spitting up blood in the process.

Internal injuries.

"Ugh, that's gross," Tia said as she approached the car behind Nathan.

"I thought I told you to stay in the car," Nathan said, whirling around, startled.

"The first thing you should realize about me is that I don't take orders very well," she said, smiling at him.

"But you're pretty good at givin' 'em, huh?" he countered.

Another loud moan from the driver put a temporary halt to their verbal sparring as they both looked at him.

"He was at the club tonight, sitting at the bar."

"I thought he looked familiar," Nathan agreed.

"I've seen him somewhere else, though. I can't put my finger on it. Before he walked out of Jimmy's, he turned and looked at where Hank and me was sittin'. I looked right at him, and I'll tell you what. Something about that dude freaked me out. I had the feelin' you'd better not fuck with him," she said quietly.

"Well, he ain't fuckin' with nobody now. He ain't got long to go."

Suddenly, the injured killer reached out and grabbed Nathan by his shirt.

"Get me out of here, punk," Marcello Baldino groaned.

"FUCK YOU!" Nathan shouted as he pulled away from the gangster's grip. "I AIN'T DOIN' SHIT FOR YO SORRY ASS. WHERE'S MY WOMAN, MOTHAFUCKA?"

The gangster groaned again.

"YOU FUCKIN' DAGOS SNATCHED HER, DIDN'T YOU?"

"I don't know nuthin about that," the bleeding man moaned, coughing up more blood in the process. "All I know is that you ripped off Don Salvatore and it's my job to make you pay."

"You better forget that, bro," Nathan said as he looked down at the dying man. "You ain't gonna make it."

"Fuck you," the killer replied as he reached out to Nathan, this time flashing metal where his hand was previously.

"LOOK OUT!" shouted Tia as she spotted the shiny chrome in the palm of his hand.

As quick as Tia saw the gangster's gun, Nathan was quicker. He raised his own handgun and fired one shot, hitting Marcello in the face. The impact of the bullet forced his head back suddenly, making a loud cracking sound as his neck broke. Blood flowed from the fresh wound like water escaping a garden hose. The huge killer trembled with one last shudder before his body went still, joining his partner in death.

Nathan and Tia stood there, frozen by the sight of Marcello "the Bear" Baldino, and what was left of Angelo "Little Vito" Arbolino. Tia stared at Marcello's open, glazed eyes, remembering his stare from the bar earlier. She couldn't bring herself to look at the mess that was "Little Vito" for more than a few seconds. When she did, her stomach turned upside down.

"I'm gonna be sick," she groaned as she raced to the nearest tree.

Nathan had been exposed to many things in his twenty-four years but never had he been forced to kill a man before. He remained still, his eyes locked on the grisly scene. Only the sound of approaching sirens broke his daze. They didn't have much time.

"Hurry up, Tia," he said as he began to go through Marcello's pockets. "We got to get the fuck out of here."

"I'm comin'," she said, stepping from behind the tree.

She wiped her mouth to get any remaining residue off her face before turning to greet Nathan.

"So who is he?" she asked as she approached the wreckage.

"Dunno yet," Nathan replied as he stuck the dead man's wallet into his pocket. He attempted to reach over the huge corpse to search

"Little Vito's" body but the remains of his face was hanging down in a revolting mixture of blood and gore that Nathan was unable to deal with. He pulled out of the car.

"Damn, that other guy's fucked up. You see what's left of his face?"

"Yeah. That's what got me."

The sound of police sirens grew louder. Nathan knew they had to leave now or risk being detained.

"Come on. Time to book."

He grabbed her hand as he led her back to the waiting Mustang. Once inside, he tossed her the dead gangster's wallet.

"Let's see what we got," he said as he shifted the car into gear. As they pulled off, he could see a small fire beginning to start under the wreckage. *It wouldn't be long before the whole thing went in flames,* he thought as he accelerated.

"His name is Marcello Baldino," Tia began reading his drivers license. "Lives in Warren. No credit cards."

She opened the billfold to expose currency. "Lots of cash."

Her eyes widened as she began to count the money.

"One, two, three, four . . . there must be a couple thousand dollars here. Look, all C notes," she said, showing him the wallet.

He took a quick glance at the wallet and then returned his eyes to the road.

"Check this out," Nathan said as he pulled out a wad of bills as big as his fist. It was wrapped tightly with a thick rubber band. "This guy was loaded."

Tia's face brightened as she anticipated the answer to her question.

"So we gonna split it?"

Nathan looked at her and smiled. He knew how hard it was to make any real money in this world. Unless you had a full-time, good-paying 9 to 5, you hustled. If you made your life on the streets, an opportunity like this was one which you didn't pass up.

"Keep whatever you got. Right now, we gotta get off the streets. We can't keep riding around like this. We got to hold up somewhere to figure our next move."

Tia continued her search of the dead killers' wallet. There were four different driver's licenses in one of the card slots. Tia had no way of knowing that those were the IDs of Marcello Baldinos' last four hits. She also found a business card for Pussycats nightclub, one of many business holdings that John Salvatore owned under the name Greektown, Inc. Tia handed the card to Nathan as he pulled into the parking lot of a twenty-four-hour party store.

"Pussycats. Yeah, I been there. It's not as fly as TJ's but it was all right."

"Check out the back," she advised.

He turned the card around to see a couple of phone numbers written on it. Both numbers were instantly familiar.

"How'd that guy get my sister's number?"

"I don't know," he answered. "But we gonna find out. Look, why don't you run inside and get us something to munch on? We gonna be on the go after some rest time and I don't know when we gonna have another chance to eat."

"I am kind of hungry," she agreed. "Plus I gotta get some mouthwash. I got a bold taste in my mouth."

"Vomit will do that to ya," he replied sarcastically.

Tia rolled her eyes as she stepped out of the car. As she walked into the store, Nathan looked again at the card. It was common knowledge throughout the city that Johnny Salvatore controlled everything which has the Greektown, Inc. emblem. The emblem was printed in small print on the card under the Pussycat logo. That wasn't what he found interesting. What stirred Nathan up was the second number. A pager number he's called before. Kay Browns' pager. The two women he deals with and both their numbers were in the dead guy's pocket.

"Why did this guy have Kay Brown's number?" he wondered aloud.

"That other number is Kay Brown's? I'd like to know that myself," Tia said as she slid back into the car.

He was ready with a quick comeback when a loud explosion in the distance altered his train of thought. It was the car in Palmer Park. Nathan and Tia looked at each other, both reflecting on the events of the last few minutes.

"Time to go," he said as he put the car in gear. "We need to settle down for a while before we make any more moves."

Tia wanted to ask him about Kay Brown's number but she held

her tongue. *Now wasn't the right time,* she concluded.

"So where we gonna go? My place?"

He shook his head.

"No, they might have it scoped out. I got a better idea. Sit back and relax. We'll get a room uptown and chill for a bit. After we rest, we'll be thinkin' clear enough to know what to do. Don't worry. We gonna find Jeri."

Tia settled back in her seat and closed her eyes.

"I'm not worried," she lied. "Just concerned. That bitch, Kay Brown, is the one who should be worried. If anything's happened to my sister, she's . . . "

Nathan reached out and touched his finger to her lips.

"Gonna answer to me."

Tia smiled, a relaxed, peaceful look coming over her face. Looking at her, Nathan began to feel confident again. Maybe, everything would work out after all. He got the upper hand on the godfather's hitmen, so anything was possible. The criminal organization now knew he wasn't some young clown who was gonna punk out. He picked up the business card and looked at it again.

"We gonna ride by Jeri's. Maybe she's there, sleep like you said. Tia?"

Her steady breathing told him she was asleep. *With any luck, Jeri's car will be parked in her usual spot,* he thought as he pointed the car towards 8 Mile Road. The deep feeling in his gut told him he was wasting his time going by her apartment, but he had to check it out. Maybe she would be there, waiting for him. Or maybe she was like his brother.

The thought of his brother's murder sent a cold, aching shudder throughout his body. Somebody was going to pay for it. He glanced at the business card again, Kay's number burning through him.

"Somebody's gonna pay."

CHAPTER FOURTEEN

The gold, 2-door Lexus coupe Kay Brown was driving was hitting a speed close to 100 mph as she flew down the Lodge freeway, on her way downtown. She pushed the CD button on the dash and the latest Missy Elliot hit filled the car with hip-hop. The car belonged to DJ Heat, her intimate friend at Jimmy D's. *Sometimes, a good blowjob gets all kinds of fringe benefits,* she thought as she remembered his words.

"Yeah baby, you can grip the ride for a bit. Don't be long, though, I gots to be on the north end after we close."

"No problem, boo," she purred. "I'll be back before your boy down there gets ready for me again," she said, looking at his crotch. When she turned on the charm, there weren't too many men who could refuse her wishes.

She glanced in her rearview mirror to see if the red Porsche, which had been following her since Jimmy's, was still on her.

"Keep comin', girl," Kay said, spotting her familiar lights bending the curve. "It's about time we hooked up again."

She recognized the red sports car as Jeri Day's. No doubt, her sister Tia called her as soon as she walked into the bar with Nathan. Her face turned into a frown as she thought of the way things ended with Hank Littlejohn. She didn't really know him that well, but she knew how much Nathan cared for him. It made her wonder for the first time if she would come out of this unscathed.

"Hey," she told herself. "It wasn't my fault. I'm just along for the ride."

But her conscience wasn't buying it.

Her mind raced back to the day five years ago when she first stepped into the Pussycats Club, hoping to get a job as a waitress. After talking to a few of the regulars, she was sure she could get a gig dancing instead. Her private show for one of the owners' business associates clinched the deal. She smiled, thinking about the night she reduced a man as large as he was to a little boy. She tied him up and spanked him until his big Italian butt was red and lined with welts. It was crazy to her, but she learned that some people needed pain to get off. And she would happily dish it out.

As long as she got paid well, of course.

She looked around the new car. She's got to get one of these, she thought.

As she approached downtown through the tunnel under Cobo Hall, she noticed the red Porsche had slowed considerably. *She was keeping her distance*, Kay thought as she stopped for the red light. Why? What was she up to?

"The hell with this bullshit," Kay exclaimed as the light turned green. She was going to settle things with Jeri once and for all.

She drove the gold sports car slowly down Jefferson, checking her rearview mirror constantly. She wanted to make sure her friend didn't lose her. Soon, she spotted her destination. It would be a good time for them to clear the air, Kay thought as she pointed her car in the direction of Belle Isle Park. It was a beautiful island located in the Detroit River, between Detroit and Canada. People would go to Belle Isle twenty-four hours to hang out, to party, or to be alone with that special someone.

Kay smiled, thinking of the many times she and Nathan had hung out on the strip. That was the long street that ran along the back of the park. All of the action happened on the strip: radio blasting, people dancing, guys trying to pick up girls, and vice versa. Kay grinned, thinking of a few successful one-nighters she's had on the island. But none of them made her feel the way she did when she was with Nathan. They would get a couple of drinks, a couple of blunts, and go to the island and stay all day. That was when everything was so simple.

She glanced into the rearview again. *Still there*, she told herself as she crossed the bridge.

Let's see what's on her mind.

Why is she going to Belle Isle at this time of the morning? Jeri asked herself as she followed the gold Lexus onto the island park. After flying down the freeway, Jeri was relieved when Kay slowed down to cruise Jefferson. At first, Jeri thought Kay was going to meet someone, but now it was obvious that she had been spotted and that she probably knew who was following her. *It was just as well,* she thought. Better to deal with her now and see how she's involved with Nathan before she confronts him.

After cruising along the strip for about a half a mile, the two cars pulled over. There were four or five other cars parked along the strip this morning, none parked close together. For making-out purposes, the farther spaced apart, the better. Only the red Porsche and the gold Lexus were parked together. As the two women left their cars, the tension in the air was unmistakable. Someone was about to get an ass-kicking. Jeri sat on the hood of her car, trying to remain calm. As she followed Kay downtown, she was convinced that as soon as they saw each other, the fight was on. But that wasn't the way she wanted it. She wanted to find out the truth about her and Nathan. If he wasn't man enough to be straight with her, she would find answers herself. She looked at Kay Brown, extending her six-foot-tall frame out of the gold sports car. Jeri forgot how tall she was.

She is very attractive, Jeri thought as she began listing reasons why Nathan would be interested in her. She dressed very provocatively. She knew that turned Nathan on.

He was always trying to get Jeri to dress sexier, but it wasn't in her nature. *God gave you a helluva body and you keep it under wraps,* he was always telling her. She could tell Kay Brown had no such inhibitions.

"What's happenin', girlfriend?" Kay greeted Jeri. "You been on my ass since I left Jimmy's."

She paused to light up a joint.

Reason number two.

Nathan loved weed and anybody who smoked it was cool for him and his business, Jeri thought. Kay extended the joint towards her.

"You wanna hit this?"

"Naw, that's all right. Kinda early for gettin' high."

"Girl, I ain't come down yet," she laughed.

Jeri looked at her and frowned. She knew Kay was trouble when she first met her and she's done nothing to make her think differently.

"Look, I'm not tryin' to hang out and be friends."

The smiling and the laughing stopped. Kay could see Jeri meant business. Okay. She was ready for it.

"You the one followin' me. You wanna tell me what's up or what?" she demanded, her attitude changing quickly.

"You wanna tell me what's happenin' with you and my man?"

Kay acted surprised, her eyes growing large.

"Your man? Girl, I got lots of friends, you'll have to be more specific."

They both knew who they were talking about. Jeri could see it in her attitude.

"Nathan Littlejohn, bitch."

Kay looked at Jeri, sensing her anger. She knew she was ready to fight. It's been a while since her last fight. When she first started at Pussycats, one of the dancers didn't appreciate her being the new girl and getting the main stage. The main stage was for the hottest one. After Kay Brown's performance, there was no doubt who that was. The jealous dancer tried to mess with her music while she was on one night. After finishing the dance, Kay Brown proceeded to use the girl's face as a toilet brush, letting her know who was in charge at Pussycats now.

She didn't have a problem after that. *Maybe it was time to let this bitch know who she was fucking with,* she thought. She smiled as she hit the joint again.

"Oh, Nathan. You were at the club tonight. I didn't see you inside, but you were somewhere. You seen us together, right?"

Silence.

"Well, let me tell you something, Miss Thang," she began. "I don't give a fuck if he's your man or not. He wants to snatch me up so we can go fuckin', that's our business. You got a problem with it, you take it up on him."

Kay took another hit of the joint and started up again before Jeri could get a word in.

"Ain't this a bitch? You gonna follow me around like you crazy or something then break on me for fuckin' what you say is your man. If your pussy ain't good enough to keep him in your bed, don't drop your shit at my feet. I know how to satisfy. That's what pisses you off."

Jeri found herself unable to speak.

Kay Brown had that effect on people. She could be seductively charming, outrageously bitchy, or brutally vicious. She could be very cruel when she wanted to be and that was her mood now.

"You think you all that," she continued. "Bitch, you ain't shit. I can get that motherfucka anytime I want him."

"That's bullshit!" Jeri finally responded. "You think I followed you 'cause I'm ready to give him to you? I seen ya'll tonight. I seen you tryin' to get up in his face and he backed off. He don't want your stankin' ass anymore."

"Bitch, you must be crazy," Kay said, her voice rising. "You seen what happened. His brother was in that car. That fucked him up. His mind was gone after that. But that's all right. I'll meet him in Palmer Park later. He'll need some more comforting when he's done with your sister."

By Jeri's facial expression, Kay knew that last lie got to her. She decided to pour it on.

"Girl, didn't you know about them? Oh yeah," she said, snapping her fingers. "They probably at Palmer Park now. If I was you, that's who I'd be pissed at. It's one thing to mess around with another woman, but it's something else to fuck around with your sister's man. I'd never put up with that sh . . . "

The palm of Jeri's hand interrupted Kay's flow of dialogue as it made hard contact with the side of her face. Kay looked at Jeri, her eyes getting misty. She put her tongue to the corner of her mouth where she had been hit, tasting blood.

The fight was on.

"Ahhhhhh!" she screamed as she rushed towards Jeri, swinging her arms wildly. "I'm gonna beat your ass, bitch!"

Doing her best "World Wrestling Babe of the Week" moves, Kay connected with a right hand to the head, causing Jeri to slump over next to her car. She followed with a swift kick to the stomach, which left Jeri on her knees, gasping for air.

"WHAT'S THE MATTER, BITCH? YOU WANT TO DISH IT OUT BUT CAN'T TAKE IT? YOU THINK YOU CAN TAKE ME, SLUT?"

She delivered another kick to the stomach, more vicious than the first. Then another. As Jeri struggled on the ground, trying to protect herself, Kay moved to Jeri's other side, delivering one more kick to the back. By the sound of her groaning, Kay figured she'd had enough. She crouched down in front of the beaten woman, breathing heavily.

"You had enough, bitch?" Kay said, breathing hard.

Jeri moaned again, this time louder.

"Good. I'm tired and ready to go. Here's something for ya."

She leaned over and spit into Jeri's face.

"You wanna throw again, you better come stronger than this. I'll kill your ass next time, scankass ho."

Kay rose from the crumpled woman and began walking away, talking over her shoulder.

"I'll tell Nathan we partied," she said as Jeri struggled to her feet, leaning on her car.

"Maybe I'll go to Palmer Park now," she gloated. "After he's done with your sister, I know he'll be ready for me. She's probably weak, like your ass so he's gonna need some good freaky love. He told me you pretty stiff. Why he's with you, I don't know. But I bring out the freak in him, you know what I'm sayin'?"

While Kay Brown was busy running her mouth, Jeri had made her way back inside her car. Opening the glovebox in her car, she found what she was looking for. She had something for Miss Brown's ass, she thought as she wiped the spittle off her face, regaining focus.

"Keep talkin', bitch," she mumbled under her breath.

Full of herself, Kay Brown did just that. After the beating she just gave Jeri Day, Kay was under the impression that she was too scared to do anything else.

She was wrong.

Once Jeri had her hands on the handle of the 9mm handgun,

momentum shifted in her favor. The pain in her back and side eased as she aimed the gun at Kay's back.

"Hey, bitch," she moaned. "Turn around."

Kay turned her head as she kept walking to her car. Her eyes got wide when she saw the gun in Jeri's hand.

"You ain't got nuthin to say now, huh?"

Kay remained silent, glaring at Jeri.

"Get your stupid ass over here."

She hesitated before a warning shot fired through the windshield of DJ Heat's new Lexus convinced her that Jeri meant business.

"You think I'm bullshittin'? Get your ass over here, NOW!"

Kay walked slowly over to Jeri's car, where she was instructed to get in the passenger's seat.

"Put the seat belt on."

Again, Kay hesitated, but the pressure from the 9mm on her head made her rethink her position. She snapped it on.

"Good decision."

Suddenly, a quick forward thrust brought the handle of the gun across the jaw of the woman in the passenger seat, knocking her unconscious instantly.

"Stupid-ass bitch. Look at you now!"

Jeri closed the door and took a moment to compose herself. Would she really have shot Kay if she had to, she wondered. The question rolled around in her mind until she realized people from the other cars were slowly approaching them.

She walked around to the driver's side of the car while keeping an eye on the crowd. She didn't have time for twenty questions. She quickly slid behind the wheel, grimacing in pain.

"We got places to go, girlfriend," she said to the unconscious woman as she gingerly snapped her seat belt over her possibly cracked ribs.

"You ready? Wait a sec, lemme fix your makeup."

She leaned over and spit into Kay Brown's face.

"Now you're ready."

After watching her newly applied makeup slide snail-like down the unconscious woman's face, Jeri day put her red two-seater into drive and took off, leaving the early-morning lovers of Belle Isle to investigate the gold Lexus with the bullet-shattered windshield.

As she drove off into the darkness, she found herself wondering about the accusations her unconscious passenger made. Could any of it be true? Why hasn't Tia called her back yet? With all that went down tonight, that surprised her.

What would she do when Kay woke up Jeri wondered as she crossed back over the bridge. Maybe Nathan's got some ideas. Soon, she would know the truth about everything Nathan's been up to lately. Funny how your life can change in a matter of moments, remembering the promises he made to her. After everything that's happened tonight, how can their relationship survive any more drama? *Hopefully, he'll have the answers I need,* she prayed as she zoomed into the city towards Palmer Park.

CHAPTER
FIFTEEN

"My Way" once again sang out from Johnny Salvatore's breast pocket. Not too many people knew his cell phone number, and those who did knew not to abuse the privilege. The person calling was in that inner circle, and he knew his call would be greatly appreciated by the boss. Nobody liked a rat, stoolie, informer, or any other adjective you could use to describe a crooked cop on "Greektown Johnny's" payroll. But that was his job at police headquarters and he was good at it.

"Yes," Johnny began. "What do you have for me? . . . WHAT? When did that happen? . . . I see . . . no, I know who's responsible . . . where? . . . Uh-huh . . . that doesn't surprise me. I seem to have a lot of business in Palmer Park lately . . . What? . . . No, no, you did fine. This is why you get paid, for quick information . . . Anything else I should know? . . . You doin' good kid. Keep it up."

Johnny Salvatore was now pissed off. It was bad enough that a young punk showed his ass by sticking his nose in to his dope business, but now he's cost him two of his best men. If word got out that some amateurs took him, people might get the idea that he was getting weak. Once that idea caught on, people might not be so willing to pay for protection. That was a huge part of his business. He still had a couple tricks up his sleeve, he thought as he pushed the buttons on the cell phone.

"Let's get back to the club, pronto," he ordered the driver. "I got a little business to take care of."

"We got problems, boss?" one of his bodyguards asked.

"I'll tell you who's got problems," the gangster growled. "That nigger Littlejohn's got problems. He thinks his brother got fucked up, he ain't seen nothin' yet. I'm gonna make that boy hurt so bad, he'll be beggin' for me to whack him."

The mobster began screaming into his phone, alerting his henchmen that he received more bad news.

"GODDAMMIT, GINO! HOW'D YOU JUST SIT THERE AND LET 'EM WALTZ OUTTA THERE? YOU GOT ROCKS IN YA BRAIN? DIDN'T I TELL YOU WHEN I LEFT, NOBODY LEAVES? GODDAMN, GINO!"

The godfather was on the verge of a heart attack.

"THAT FUCKIN' MORON LET COLLAZO AND GARBARINI WALK RIGHT OUTTA THERE."

The two gangsters in the front of the car looked at each other. They had seen their boss trip out like this before and neither of them wanted to be on the receiving end of his latest tirade.

"I'm gonna have his balls for breakfast," he said, calming down. "Turn the car around."

The driver made a sharp U-turn, smoking his tires and cutting off what little traffic there was.

"Where we goin', boss?"

"It's time to finish this bullshit," the crime lord said. "After we take care of Littlejohn, we'll find Mike and Frankie and tie up those loose ends."

He pushed a button and the wet bar appeared. He was about to turn up his sixth scotch of the night when he caught the eyes of his driver in the rearview mirror.

"WHAT THE FUCK ARE YOU LOOKIN' AT? GET THIS CAR MOVIN'!"

The dark sedan accelerated quickly, sending the trio of killers into the darkness. Next stop, the Palmer Park apartment of Nathan Littlejohn.

*   *   *

Mike Garbarini reread the letters over again. What Frank told him was making sense. It was starting to fit. As many questions were appearing in Mike's head, many were also being answered.

"So you think Johnny and Tony were in on some kinda of conspiracy to keep me in jail? Why? How would that benefit them?"

Frank knew he'd better convince Mike that he knew what he was talking about. If Johnny finds out he knows about Tony, it would be all over for him. John Salvatore wouldn't take any chances on the possibility of his being implicated. Frank knew John would have him killed. That's how he worked.

"With you in jail not makin' noise, the real killer didn't worry about the truth comin' out. They had their killer. The cops wouldn't waste time on a murder case that was solved."

Frank looked closely at Mike, trying to read him. Those years in prison taught Mike how to hide his real feelings behind a stoic face. He didn't want to be figured out or helped. He wanted to be believed. He needed to be believed. If he could put it all together, finally . . .

"All right," Frank said, relaxing for the first time since they arrived at the office. "I did some more digging after I found out about Tony. Mr. Jenkins was a nosy old bastard. He was the one who found out everything about Tony. At first, I wondered why he did it, all the digging, taking a chance like he did. But you know what? Hate is a helluva motivator. The old dude was tough. You couldn't work for John and not be able to take his shit. He hated Johnny. Johnny didn't realize how much he hated him. And John didn't realize how important that land was to him. You can learn a lot from a person after workin' with them for a couple of decades. You learn what makes them tick. Somehow, old man Jenkins found out about John's payoffs and figured a way to find more."

Frank took the letters from Mike and put them in his pocket. After placing the book back into the bookcase, Frank continued with his story.

"I think Jenkins got in touch with Tony and convinced him that our boy was going to stop payments. I don't know why but he bought it.

The next day, Tony called John and threatened to go to the New York family."

Frank could tell Mike was getting impatient. He needed more convincing. "While Tony was livin' in New York, he made a few connections on his own that John apparently wasn't aware of."

"It didn't take Johnny long to decide he was through getting blackmailed. It didn't bother him payin' Tony all these years. It was in his best interest to keep Tony away. He probably thought Tony wanted more than just money. I think he maybe wanted something John didn't want to give him."

"Something like what?" Mike asked.

"I dunno," Frank said with a shrug of his shoulders. "Something John loves more than money. Power?"

Mike sat up, surprised by what he just heard.

"You talked to him?"

Frank didn't answer. "That's why you think Tony was in a position to challenge John for power."

Frank hesitated before he continued.

"All right. I did go to New York to see him. After I talked to Jenkins, I knew seein' Tony would answer a lot of my questions. But I was too late. John got to him first. He's dead."

A look of anger flashed across Mike's face for a minute before he spoke to the pizza maker.

"So now, Tony's dead."

"Yes."

"So how you know it was John? This don't prove John had him killed."

Frank shook his head.

"Wrong. It proves that when Tony decided to cross John, he ended up dead. Just like the butler. Besides, not everything is in that letter."

He leaned forward, putting emphasis on the next bit of information.

"The old man told me he listened in when Tony called John on the phone. Tony said if he didn't want a certain firearm to show up at a certain police precinct thirty years after they stopped lookin' for it, he better kick those payments back on. That's when John had him killed, I bet."

"Why would he kill him now after all this time? He still didn't have the gun. He wouldn't take that chance unless he knew he could lay his hands on it."

"Maybe he got tired of payin' Tony all that money. He never liked nobody gettin' the best of him. I think he somehow got wind of the old man makin' contact with Tony. That's why he got rid of his son. He thought he could make the old man talk and when he wouldn't tell him about Tony or what he knew about the gun, he lost his temper and killed him. The crackhead son didn't know anything about the gun, but Johnny didn't know that. Once he finds out about how much I know, I'll be next. He finds out you suspect him and you'll be dead. The only thing holdin' him back is finding the gun."

Mike thought about what Frank just said. It was making more sense to him as he thought about it.

"Why did he tell you all of this?"

"I don't know why he felt he could trust me. He knew I respected him. Whenever Johnny came around and Jenkins was with him, he liked to make a big deal of it, like havin' a servant made him royalty or something. Jenkins was a proud man and it irked Johnny that he couldn't take his dignity. I was one of the few guys hangin' around that didn't look down on him. The family used blacks for different menial jobs, but they didn't respect the work they did. I did. I always respected him."

"So," the ex-con began. "Where's that leave us? He didn't tell you where the gun is, did he?"

"If I had the gun by now, I would've had Johnny's balls, Mike. No, he didn't tell me where it was. But he did tell me something interesting."

"What?"

Frank thought quickly about how much more he should tell Mike. He hadn't planned on telling him this much, but once he started, he knew he had to satisfy most of the questions.

"He told me his son's friend had come up with the idea of hittin' Johnny's crack houses. He wanted to get that bullshit off the streets and out of the neighborhood. It killed Jenkins to see his son strung out like that, so he decided to do what he could, from the inside."

Frank chuckled, thinking about the old man's own private war on drugs.

"That old man had balls. Big balls."

"Yeah," Mike said. "I believe you. So what else?"

"He told me the friend had a Bible just like this. And the old man's was passed down from his great-grandfather. To see one that's identical, that must have impressed him."

"So you think he was tryin' to tell you somethin'?"

Frank shrugged his shoulders again, sighing deeply.

"I dunno. Maybe. He liked to talk, but it didn't have to mean anything. Still, he had a funny look in his eyes when he told me about it. He made a point of me knowin' about the Bible being identical to his."

"So you know the guy?"

"No. Never met him. All I know is that he stays in Palmer Park and his name is Littlejohn.

A troubled look came over Mike Garbarini's face.

"You know I told you Johnny caught up to one of your buddies? His name was Littlejohn."

Frank Collazo almost dropped his drink when he heard the name.

Could they be too late? John could have the proof needed to get away with murder again. Thinking about all of "Greektown Johnny's" victims over the years got Frank Collazo pissed. He was determined not to add his name to the list.

"Come on," Frank said, rising from his desk. "We got to get to Palmer Park. Maybe Johnny hasn't gotten anything out of him. Maybe what we're lookin' for is at Littlejohn's place."

"I don't think John talked to him," Mike said, following Frank out of the office. "They blew up the car with him in it. John said he wanted to make an example out of him, but he had something special planned for the leader. My guess is the leader and the Bible guy are the same Littlejohn. That's the one who can help us, if we find him before John does."

"Tell me something I don't know," Frank snapped. "He's been doggin' me for years, but now, things are different. I got the jump on him."

With that, the two men left the downtown high-rise for what appears to be a meeting with fate in Palmer Park.

CHAPTER SIXTEEN

"Tia, Tia," the voice called out in the darkness. "Tia, wake up, we're here."

The sleeping woman came out of her fog to instantaneous alertness. Recognizing their location achieved that.

"Are you crazy? Why would you come back here?" she said, looking at the entrance of the Palmer Park apartment building.

"There's nobody around. I checked," Nathan said, opening the car door.

"Besides, I needed to pick up a couple of things. We won't stay long. Long enough for me to clean up a little. Then I'll take us to get a room."

Tia looked at him, her eyebrows raised.

"Well, we can't stay here."

"We can go to my place," Tia said.

"That ain't no safer than if we stayed here. We haven't heard from your sister so I have to assume they know about everybody who was involved and where we all live."

"We weren't involved."

He looked at her like she was crazy for a minute before he continued.

"Girl, ya'll involved now. You think they don't have all of us under the eye now? We all in the crosshairs."

She thought about it and decided he was right.

"All right, we can get a room. But no funny business. You my sister's man and I don't play that shit."

"Ain't you full of yourself! To chill in. A room to chill in. I gotta think," he said, getting out.

"Is sex always the only thing on your mind?"

"Yeah, right. That's why you were with Kay Brown tonight. Y'all was going to the library to study," she said, dripping sarcasm.

"Look," Nathan said, slamming the car door. "That's over. I told you that. My relationship with her is in the past. Besides, it wasn't a big deal. It was just sex, that's all."

"That's all?" she said, slamming the door as she followed him.

Her voice began to rise as she became agitated.

"In this day and age, there is no such thing as just sex."

"Hey, I used protection. I always used protection."

"That's not the point. You shouldn't have been with her in the first place."

When they got to the front door of the apartment building, Nathan turned and faced her. They had a few things they needed straightening out.

"First of all," he began. "You have no idea what me and Jeri's relationship is like. We break up to make up. Sometimes, I do things that she don't dig and vice versa. It ain't perfect, nobody's is. I've made mistakes and she knows about most of them. But I already told you, Kay and me are a thing of the past. Why bring it up here?"

Tia looked at him intently. He could be very persuasive she thought as she found herself gazing into his light brown eyes. Very persuasive.

"Come on," she said, breaking the spell. "Let's go inside. We don't need to linger in the street."

As he held the door open for her, she brushed past him, inadvertently making contact with her 38's.

His eyes were drawn to her ample cleavage as he felt the light touch across his chest. She felt his eyes on her and paused in front of him, sensing his arousal.

"So," she said softly. "Where is your mind now?"

Embarrassed, he looked away quickly and started for the stairs.

"Come on," he said over his shoulder. "We got things to do."

She smiled at him, acknowledging the attraction his six-foot-two, muscular frame seemed to have for her. After admiring his physique, she ran up the stairs behind him.

Unknown to both of them, they both had a set of eyes watching their every move, also acknowledging the mutual attraction.

The parts of the conversation she heard was enough to make Jeri Day's head spin.

"I can't believe it," she said, stunned. "He just took my sister up to his fuckin' apartment."

She looked over at the still unconscious woman, imagining all the different sexual encounters they must have had.

"You've been up there, in his bed. Haven't you?"

She shook the woman a few times, but she remained out. She looked back at the now empty doorway.

"I can't fuckin' believe it. My own sister, stabbin' me in the back."

Tears filled her eyes as the image of Tia and Nathan's naked bodies flooded her thoughts. In her mind, they were rolling around his king-sized waterbed, exploring each other's bodies until every spot was discovered. She shivered, thinking of Nathan's tongue in her sister's ear, making it's way down to her open mouth, her awaiting breasts, and beyond.

"I'm gonna kick that bitch's ass," she announced as she grabbed the gun from under her seat and got out of the car gingerly, her ribs still sore from the fight she had earlier. As she closed the car door, she did so quietly. She wasn't going to make a sound to tip them off about her arrival. She leaned on the car, looking up at his fifth-floor apartment window, waiting for the right time. After about five minutes, the lights from the front room were joined by a faint glow illuminating from the second window.

The bedroom window.

They weren't wasting any time.

"Bastard," she muttered. "He thinks he can do whatever the fuck he wants."

She leaned over and spoke into the closed eyes of Kay Brown.

"After I take care of this nigga and this bitch, we'll see how much more you can handle. See ya!"

She quickly, but quietly, walked over to the apartment's front door. Reaching into her pocket, she pulled out a set of keys that Nathan had no knowledge of.

One day, he locked his keys in his apartment and it cost him thirty dollars for the super to let him in. After driving her crazy bitching about it for two days, Jeri took his keys and had copies made. She had meant to give them to him but they got into an argument about commitment and amnesia kicked in.

It was going to take two men in white jackets to commit him, he told her.

She didn't find it funny, but now she knew why.

He was unable to commit to any woman. Her, her sister, Kay Brown, who knew how many others he was bedding. *Those days would be over soon*, she thought as she put the key in the lock and turned it. She had never used the keys before and hoped they would open with no hassle.

"Shit," she said to herself.

The lock was stuck.

As she tried turning the keys to force the lock open, a voice from the other side of the door cried out, startling her.

"Goddammit, stop tryin' to turn the lock. Your key is jammed. What do you wanna do, break it off?"

It was the irritating drone of the super, Mr. Carlton Simpson. Mr. Simpson was seventy-two, a widower who had secretly hoped his wife of 50 years would die so he could travel, live off their life savings and start a new life. He got his wish two years ago. However, due to his stubbornness and stupidity, he ignored his wife's advice to get decent life insurance, so the savings he so desperately coveted went to pay for her months in the hospice and ultimately, her burial. He was forced to continue his bitter existence trying to live on what he made as apartment superintendent. Deservedly so.

"What you tryin' to do? Oh, hello, Miss."

"Sorry, Mr. Simpson," she said in a whispering tone. "I didn't mean to break anything."

"Oh, that's all right," he said, leering at her through his thick bifocals, his eyes locked on her 34-24-36 figure. He licked his cracked, dry lips as he opened the security door for her. "Glad to be of service to such a lovely young lady."

She hurriedly walked past him, trying to avoid his lusty stare.

"You going to see Littlejohn, eh? Kinda early for a visit."

"Well," she began. "We were supposed to have dinner last night but I canceled our date because of work. He was a little upset."

That sounded convincing.

"Young love," he said, walking up behind her. "I remember it well."

He was standing so close to her she could smell the whiskey as his hot breath covered the back of her neck.

Suddenly, he pulled her back to him, his hardness pressing against her.

"Forget about him," the old man whispered in her ear. "I got somethin' for ya."

"Motherfucka!" she said, trying to pull away. "You better let me loose. I don't play this bullshit." Like her sister, Jeri was tough. Growing up in the Herman's Garden's projects prepared her with the hardness that her life required.

"Sure you do," he said, pressing against her harder. "You got that low-cut shirt on showin' half your tits. Your pants are tighter than a Jew holdin' a buck. It's almost daybreak and you here to see Littlejohn for some bonin'. Ya'll always goin' at it. You tryin' to tell me this ain't a booty call?"

"Well . . . "

"That's all right," he said, laughing as he released her from his iron grip. "I was just foolin' with ya."

"Oh," she said, forcing a weak laugh. He was stronger than he looked.

"No need to tell Nathan about this, huh?"

She forced a smile, wishing she could waste this old man. But she had more important things to do.

"It'll be our little secret."

The dirty old man winked.

"I knew you was okay. Tell Nathan I said hey. He's just gettin' in not too long ago."

Jeri froze, hoping he would give her the right answer to her questions.

"Did you see him? Was he alone?"

"No, I didn't see him. Heard him going upstairs though. Everybody else takes the elevators. He loves to run the stairs. Keeps him in shape, he tells me. When I was young . . . "

"Was he alone?" she interrupted.

"I didn't hear him talkin' to nobody. I think he was."

Good. He didn't see them together. She might just be able to pull this off.

"Thanks, Mr. Simpson," she said, easing her way to the elevator. "I'll see you later."

"If things don't work out, come have a drink," he said, winking.

Thankfully, the old elevator was waiting for her. She pushed the button for the fifth floor and put her hand in her jacket pocket, griping the handle of her 9mm handgun as the door closed.

"I might just do that."

As Jeri Day rode the elevator up to the fifth floor, plans continued to form in her mind. She was convinced that her sister and her man betrayed her and there was no forgiving such a deplorable act. She only needed to see it with her own eyes. She held a small ray of hope that it wasn't true, but her mind continued down its negative path. If it wasn't a lie, she knew her life would change. She wouldn't allow them the satisfaction and pleasure of enjoying each other. Somebody wasn't going to see the next sunrise. Her heart began to beat faster. She started to perspire as the realization of her hidden thoughts soaked her body with an icy coldness that she'd never felt before. She shivered as the unfamiliar emotion called hate invaded her brain like a life-threatening disease. Somebody was going to die tonight.

Those thoughts of revenge, betrayal, and death weren't confined to the brain of Jeri Day. They also clouded the minds of the two men in the dark 1988 Buick sedan that pulled up in front of 19321 Covington Drive a few minutes ago. They also had business with the occupants of the fifth-floor apartment.

As they sat in the car preparing a few rounds of ammunition for their weapons, the thought that someone else was preparing an assault on the same apartment didn't escape them. In fact, they were counting on it. Where else would "Greektown Johnny" be going to collect the debts of this bloody evening?

"You sure he's gonna show up here?" the passenger asked the man behind the wheel as he loaded his .44 magnum.

Frank Collazo, restaurateur, civic leader, and the driver of the Buick, was checking the contents of the .45 automatic Mike Garbarini had given him.

"I bet big money on it. You said he got to one of the Littlejohns. The wrong one, I hope. If he's still lookin', his search will bring him here."

"How do you know he ain't been here yet?" the ex-con questioned.

"He's countin' on you to have his back. He would've called to have you meet him here, if he wasn't suspicious about our reconnection. And I don't think he is."

"So we gonna just waltz in there and explain to the homeboys that we not connected with the mob, that we got a personal score to settle with Johnny, and they should help us out?"

"Yeah, that should do it," he said with some light sarcasm tossed in. He hoped to lighten Mike's mood. They used to joke around a lot in the old days. A thousand years ago. "Seriously, if the old man was as smart as I think he was, he might have told the Littlejohns to be expecting me with the letters," he said, patting his breast pocket.

The ex-convict nodded in agreement as he checked his handgun again. They couldn't afford any mistakes and after twenty-seven years of waiting, he wasn't about to make any.

Mike looked over at Frank as he nervously checked and rechecked his gun.

"Don't worry," he said, watching the businessman wipe his sweaty forehead for the eighth time. "If this checks out, we'll be holdin' all the cards and John will have to come clean. That's what I want, to hear him admit he set me up. Whoever else is involved, I also want. I don't care who it is."

Frank stared at the man he knew well almost thirty years ago, but barely recognized now.

"Yeah, well, if somebody else let you rot in jail besides Johnny, they deserve whatever they get," he agreed. "Just one problem. How we gonna get in there? I'm a businessman, not a B & E expert."

The ex-con reached under his seat and pulled out a small leather case. He opened the case to reveal an assortment of tools, many of which would be recognized by law enforcement officials and criminals alike as the tools of the trade for those involved in the fine art of breaking and entering.

"Not a problem."

The two men continued their final preparations in silence. Though it wouldn't be long before they were ready to face the drama, both of them were unaware that the drama would be unfolding sooner than they planned. Not only because of the presence of the young lady whose pain was controlling her mind, but the fact that the dark sedan carrying Detroit's number one gangster had already arrived, parked at the rear of the building, out of sight. Soon, the quiet of Palmer Park would be no more.

CHAPTER SEVENTEEN

"What do you want to drink?" Nathan asked the woman who was sitting on the black leather couch. "I got Absolut and a little bit of white wine."

"You got any red pop?"

He opened the refrigerator door to a half-carton of spoiled milk, a couple of beers, some old pizza, and a corned-beef sandwich with two bites taken out.

"Nope. Got some beer."

"All right, that'll work."

Nathan grabbed the beers, a couple of paper plates off the top of the fridge, and the corned-beef sandwich. He brought the cold drinks into the living room, where he deposited them on the coffee table in front of the relaxed Tia Day. She had taken her shoes off and was stretched across the comfortable couch.

"Here," he said, putting the unbitten half of the sandwich and the chips she'd picked up from the store on the paper plate. He popped open the beer can and set it in front of the sleepy-eyed woman.

"You need to eat something," he said as she inspected the sandwich cautiously.

"How old is this?" she asked as she ran the sandwich under her nostrils.

"I got it three weeks ago, from the deli on Six Mile," he sarcastically replied.

She looked at her host, then at the sandwich again before she took a small bite. Her second bite told him the sandwich was fine. "Smart-ass," she smiled back.

"You eat and relax for a bit while I get some of my things together." He turned to go into the bedroom.

"You not gonna be long, are you? You know we don't need to be here," she said in between bites.

"No longer than I have to be," he called from his room.

He needed to shower and change clothes. The shirt he had on had the smell of smoke, sending the fate of his brother back into the front of his mind.

He ripped the shirt off his body, sending the buttons scattering on the hardwood floor.

"I'll be out in a minute," he called out as he slid his FUBU jeans down. "I need to take a shower."

"What?" Tia said, rising from the couch suddenly. She crossed the small front room over to the bedroom door. "We don't have time for that," she said matter-of-factly. "We're supposed to be lookin' for my sister."

"Relax. I won't be long."

She started to say something when the sound of the shower cut her off. *Fine,* she decided as she resumed her position on the couch.

This was the first time she'd been in Nathan's apartment. *It was exactly the way Jeri described it,* Tia thought as she looked around the room.

African art hung from the cream-colored walls. The black leather couch had a matching love seat that sat in the corner, opposite a five-foot-long aquarium that was filled with very large goldfish. She walked over to the aquarium and bent over to get a closer look. As she inspected the fish tank, one of the fish charged the glass wall, ramming into it. As she instinctively pulled back, her memory kicked in, reminding her of something her sister once shared with her about the aquarium's inhabitants. They weren't goldfish. They were piranha.

Thinking about her sister started Tia worrying again. She spotted the phone and decided to try Jeri one more time. Again no luck.

Maybe, she's got her pager turned on now, she said to herself as she began to push the buttons.

Then she heard it.

She turned quickly. It was a faint sound. She looked around. *What was that? It seemed to be coming from the hallway.*

A small click.

What was that sound? She couldn't figure it out until she saw the doorknob on the front door. It was turning.

Slowly.

As Tia backed towards the lone bedroom, perspiration exploded on her body. Someone was trying to open the front door.

Tia opened the door slowly, then quietly entered the bedroom, closing the door behind her. She had to get Nathan before whoever it was entered the apartment. She stepped urgently to the bathroom door. The water was still running. "Nathan," she said softly. "Nathan." Again no answer. She turned the warm doorknob to the bathroom and pushed the door open slowly. Steam flooded the small bedroom as Tia cracked open the door.

Standing naked, dripping wet, Nathan turned suddenly to find Tia, her eyes automatically drawn to his manhood.

For a brief moment, which seemed longer, there was nothing but the sound of running water to break the silence. Nathan made no move to cover himself as he reached over and picked up a towel. He watched Tia's eyes looking him up and down as he began to dry off.

"You enjoyin' yourself?" he asked, snapping her out of her daze.

"There's somebody tryin' to get in," she whispered.

The excitement he thought he saw in her eyes a second ago was actually fear.

Nathan held his finger up to his lips, signaling for Tia to be quiet. She nodded slowly, watching him open the drawer of the vanity and pull out a pistol. From experience, Nathan learned to keep his guns handy. A customer of his had a jealous boyfriend on the doorstep, accusing him of trying to seduce his woman while he was downstairs in the car, waiting. Unknown to her boyfriend, she didn't have any money and Nathan didn't give credit.

So they came to a mutual agreement.

Because of a few previous dealings when she was low on cash, he knew she gave a helluva blowjob. As it was, the hotheaded boyfriend punked out when he saw the gun in Nathan's waistband when he came up to inquire about why their transaction was taking so long. That particular night, he had his Walther PPK semiautomatic. He only had to use it once before, and it proved very effective. The events of the past twenty-four hours told him he would need the .38 caliber pistol.

"Go into the bedroom and hide behind the bed," he said, wrapping himself in a towel. "Don't make a sound until you hear my voice."

She nodded as she crept into the bedroom.

As she crouched behind the bed, the steam from the bathroom began making it almost impossible to see. The hardwood floor creaked as she heard Nathan leaving the bathroom to go to the front room. Except for the sound of the running water coming from the bathroom, it was quiet.

Then she heard it. A loud, heavy, thud.

The sound a body makes when it hits the floor.

What happened, and who was in the apartment with them?

Maybe, Nathan took care of the intruder and he was coming to tell her it was under control. The sweat from her fear combined with the steam from the shower began to make her feel uncomfortably hot. She didn't know how much more she could take when she heard the unmistakable creak of the floor again.

Someone was in the room with her.

She remembered Nathan's instructions about waiting before making a move, but the heat and the humidity was making that impossible. She had to make her move now.

As she slowly rose from the side of the bed, she could barely make out the doorway leading to the front room.

The humid fog made the bedroom cloudy so she figured now was her chance to escape. She figured wrong.

She barely made it halfway to the door when a sudden force came crashing down onto her head. Tia hit the floor hard, landing with the similar thud she heard a few seconds before. Fighting a losing battle with consciousness, she could barely make out the silhouette of a woman.

"Kay Brown, you stankin' bitch . . . " she moaned as she felt herself slipping into darkness. Her vision faded quickly as a familiar face looked down on her.

*   *   *

The two men entered the Palmer Park apartment building of Nathan Littlejohn at 4:30 A.M. without incident. Checking the mailbox, they learned of his location on the fifth floor and proceeded to the elevator. *Hopefully, things would go smoothly,* Frank Collazo thought as he looked up at the lit numbers, indicating their rise.

Mike Garbarini took his .44 Magnum out of his shoulder holster as the bell sounded, announcing their arrival at the fifth floor.

"Why you got that gun out?" Frank asked his grim partner. "I told you, there should be no problem."

"'Cause your homeboy's brother was just blown up tonight by the mob, and he might just be ready to take his shit out on the next two Italians he sees, no matter what their intentions."

Frank looked at him for second before pulling out his own gun.

"I see your point."

Apartment 520. That was the one they were looking for.

The hallway was dimly lit, which made reading the small numbers on the doors difficult.

"This way," Mike directed with the point of his gun.

The pizza man nodded, then silently followed. The apartment they were seeking was just ahead on the left, facing the street. They could hear the faint sound of music through the dimness as they approached the apartment.

Then they froze, as if on cue from some unseen movie director.

In the lock on the door of apartment 520 was a set of keys.

Everybody at one time or another have entered their apartment or house and forgotten their keys in the door. But *tonight,* that wouldn't have happened to Nathan Littlejohn.

Something was wrong and they both could feel it.

Without saying a word, Michael Garbarini signaled his partner to step over to the opposite side of the doorway before he attempted to gain entry. Frank nodded and complied.

With his back to the wall, Mike reached across to turn the key as slowly and quietly as he could. The light click of the cylinder told him it was unlocked. He again silently signaled his partner, indicating that they would go on three. Frank made the sign of the cross and kissed the crucifix around his neck, then nodded, acknowledging his readiness.

On the third wave of the gun, Mike grabbed the doorknob and turned, pushing the door slightly. It swung open slowly, letting a blast of humidity into the hallway. The two men peered into the apartment, guns ready.

Empty.

The music was coming from the other room in the apartment.

The bedroom.

Mike slid the keys out of the lock and put them in his pocket. He looked at Frank, and then entered the apartment, with the short, nervous man behind him.

Frank slowly closed the door while Mike quietly made his way across the room to the cracked door of the bedroom. A light flow of steam escaped into the outer living area.

Someone left the shower on too long, Mike thought as he felt the perspiration on the door. Maybe they were too late. Frank eased his portly frame over to the cracked door, as Mike was ready to open it.

Suddenly, they stopped as they heard a woman's voice come from the room.

She was talking to someone but neither of them heard any response.

"Hot in here, isn't it?" the female voice asked. "You guys want me to open a window?"

No response, then footsteps. The sound of a window sliding open. The two men looked at each other as the one-sided conversation continued.

"Why ya'll lookin' at me like that? I'm not the one who fucked up!"

The woman was obviously pissed off and she was letting someone know about it.

"Guess I was a fool to trust you. I thought you hurt me with your womanizing, but that was nothin' compared to tonight."

WHACK! Someone just got slapped.

"And you. How could you do this to me? We're blood. We're

supposed to stand for each other. You ain't done nothin' but play me. For this nigga. Well, I'll tell you what. You can have his punk ass."

The footsteps moved around the room constantly. They could tell she was becoming agitated.

"I seen ya'll at Jimmy's. Yeah, I was there when Hank got killed too. I seen you with your bitch-ho girlfriend, Kay Brown. Yeah, mothafucka, I seen IT ALL. Don't it matter that your brother was KILLED TONIGHT? You couldn't do shit but come fuck my sister after fallin' out with that other slut? We were supposed to be startin' fresh today, but YOU FUCKED ALL THAT UP!"

At the sound of the names, the two men eavesdropping in the next room got ready to charge in. Why weren't the other two responding?

"Couldn't be happy with me. You had to go tear out my heart! With my sister. MY SISTER!" she screamed.

Nathan Littlejohn sounded like a lowlife, Frank thought. He almost wished he didn't need his help.

"So, Tia, you wanted my man. Let's see how much you want him with his dick blown off."

With that announcement, Frank pushed the door open.

"HOLD IT, LADY! DON'T MAKE A MOVE!"

The scene looked like one of those crime dramas that come on late-night cable, with lots of sex and violence.

Tied to the bed, spread-eagled, was Nathan Littlejohn. He was naked except for a towel draped across his midsection.

There was a washcloth shoved in his mouth, preventing him from speaking. Over across the room sat a woman, tied to a chair. There was a piece of cloth stuck in her mouth also. Her eyes were red from crying and her face was streaked with mascara. Nathan's eyes grew wide as he saw the two men standing there, each holding a gun. Being tortured by his disgruntled lover was beginning to look good to him as opposed to dealing with what appeared to be the mob. Either way, he was in deep shit.

Jeri turned around, startled. Before she could react, the taller of the two men charged her, grabbed her arm and snatched her gun from her hand. As she started to open her mouth in protest, the tall man raised his arm up and slapped her across the face. The short, fat man stepped in between them.

"Come on, Mike, that wasn't necessary, was it?"

"Fuck that bitch. She was ready to pop him," his partner explained. "He's no use to us if he's dead."

"She's got a good reason, don't you think?"

The tall man glared at the scared woman for a minute before relenting.

"Go sit down and shut up," he ordered.

She quickly complied.

As Jeri took a seat in the corner of the room, Frank approached the waterbed. Nathan started squirming again, trying to get loose. He didn't have much luck this time either, as the short man sat on the edge of the bed, looking at him, shaking his head. Mike kept his eyes on the girls.

"Maybe I should've let her finish you off," he began. "From what I heard, you deserve to lose your nuts. Sleepin' with your old lady's sister."

The fat man continued scolding Nathan like a schoolboy while he frantically shook his head, defending himself with protests that came out as moans. The woman in the chair began to moan as well.

"Shut up," the tall man ordered.

Her moaning quickly changed to a barely audible whimpering.

"Okay, my friend, let's get down to business. You need my help right now and I'm not talkin' about your lady friend there. You should be thanking your lucky stars we arrived when we did."

Frank looked at his partner and smiled. Mike kept the same grim look on his face that he'd been wearing all evening.

"Before I take this out of your mouth, there's a couple of things you need to understand. Number one, I hope you got what we're lookin' for, 'cause if you don't, we're gonna leave you here to deal with your girl. Number two, we have some associates that you've pissed off a few hours ago who really want to see you. It wouldn't be a problem to call 'em up and let 'em know you're all tied up with no plans to leave."

Nathan shook his head again, his eyes pleading.

"And number three," Frank said as he reached into his pocket. "I hope for your sake, these letters mean something to you."

Frank opened the papers and held them in front of Nathan. As he looked them up and down, a look of recognition, then relief, seemed to come over his face. The man called Frank took the wad of cloth out of his mouth, allowing him to breathe easily. His breath came in quick bursts as he realized he dodged a bullet for the second time tonight.

"GIRL, YOU MUST BE OUT YOUR FUCKIN' MIND," he exploded at the angry woman in the corner.

"Fuck you and that slut sister of mine," came the cool reply.

"Ain't shit happen'n' between us. Your mind is fucked up, that's what's wrong. How you gonna come in *my crib* and fuck me like this?"

Nathan lifted his head off the bed, looking at Frank. "Untie me so I can ... "

"So you can what?" Frank interrupted.

"So I can make this crazy bitch of mine understand this situation."

"Fuck you!" Jeri piped in.

"FUCK THIS!" Mike exploded. "WE DON'T HAVE TIME FOR THIS MICKEY MOUSE BULLSHIT!"

Everybody in the room got quiet except for Tia, as she continued to protest through her gagged mouth.

"Shut up!" Mike ordered.

Silence.

Frank stood up and walked over towards Tia, where he stopped and removed her gag.

"This is very entertaining," Frank began as he turned to face Nathan. "I'd love to stay and hear you talk your way out of this mess. But," he said, pointing to his partner, "my friend is right. We don't have time to stay here and play Ricki Lake."

He walked back over to Nathan and sat on the bed.

"I hear you got an old Bible that I might be interested in. I'd like to see it."

The connection slapped Nathan upside the head, like Moe use to slap Curly. "You old man Jenkins' friend, ain't you?"

Frank shrugged his shoulders in response.

"More like acquaintances. In any event, he trusted me with a little knowledge about what you boys were plannin'. He knew ya'll was takin' a big risk hittin' those crack houses and he wanted to give ya'll a little somethin' extra, just in case. That's where we come in."

"So you ain't mob?"

"We'll be worse if you don't have what we want," Mike answered.

Nathan looked over at Mike. He meant business. For him, this was a personal issue.

"I got what you want. Untie me and I'll get it for ya."

"NO!" Jeri protested. "Don't trust that bastard. There's nothin' he can do for you!"

"SHUT UP!" You have no clue what you're talkin' about."

Frank looked at his partner, who gave a slight nod of his head. He then reached into his pocket and tossed something over to Frank. It was a switchblade knife.

The short, overweight man caught the knife with one hand, and then put his gun into his pocket. He opened the knife, revealing five inches of gleaming metal.

It was very sharp.

He sat back on the bed, looking at Nathan the whole time. Nathan was silent, keeping his eye on the shining blade.

"Now," Frank began, "it wouldn't be smart to try anything. My partner isn't as trusting as I am so any suspicious moves could result in serious problems for you and your girlfriends."

He began to cut the torn sheets that were tied around his ankles, then up to his wrists. After cutting his left arm free, Frank reached across and cut the other bind, setting him loose. Nathan sat up in his waterbed, rubbing his wrists, glaring at Jeri, who returned his stare.

"Can I put some clothes on first?" Nathan asked.

"Sure," Frank replied. "I've got no desire to see your Johnson swingin' while we're takin' care of business."

Nathan slid off the king-sized bed and walked over to his dresser to find some briefs. As he walked across the room, Jeri turned her head and watched her sister, whose eyes followed the naked body of Nathan Littlejohn.

Tia caught her sister's stare and returned the look, equally angry.

"What about me?" she asked her captives. "Aren't you gonna untie me?"

Frank again looked at his partner, who shook his head slowly.

"Sorry, princess," he said. "My partner don't think that's a good idea. Give us a few minutes and we'll see what happens."

Jeri smiled at her sister, enjoying her momentary victory.

"And you, wildcat," Frank said, wiping her face blank. "Don't try nothing or you'll face trouble like never before. You get what I'm sayin'?"

Jeri nodded. Then smiled at her sister again.

"She's gonna face trouble, all right," Nathan said, rubbing his head where Jeri had struck him earlier, revealing a small patch of blood. He looked over at his girlfriend, who smiled at him sweetly.

"All right," Frank started. "Let's get down to it. We ain't got all day."

Nathan slipped on a pair of briefs while giving Jeri another hard stare before turning his attention to Frank.

"Come with me."

Frank looked over at Mike, who was staring at both women, a hungry, lustful glaze in his eyes. He was undressing them in his mind.

"Can you handle this?" Frank asked his partner, reading his thoughts.

"Oh yeah," he responded. "I'll find something to amuse myself with." He smiled for the first time since entering the apartment.

"Maybe I'll let these two slug it out and the winner gets me."

Nathan looked over at Mike.

"If anything happens . . . "

Click.

The sound of a gun being cocked.

"Save it, Romeo," Frank said, his gun magically reappearing in his hand. "You're in no position to issue ultimatums."

He glanced over at the two women, who suddenly had a new problem that ended their hostilities.

"There'll be no problem, unless they make one."

Nathan hesitated for a moment, but a slight nudge of the .45 made any risky thoughts disappear.

"Let's go."

The two men went into the other room, with Nathan leading the way. Frank closed the door behind them while the two women looked on, helpless.

"Nathan. NATHAN!" Jeri called out to him from the bedroom. "DON'T LEAVE US IN HERE! NATHAN!"

"DON'T WORRY!" he called out. "EVERYTHING'S GONNA BE FINE. I WON'T BE LONG."

He looked at Frank again, anger building in his eyes.

"I already owe you guys for my brother. Your boy hurts my friends and payback's gonna be twice as hard."

"Relax, kid," Frank replied as he sat on the couch. "You're overestimating my influence as a local wise guy."

He pointed to the bruises on his face.

"I didn't get these because I'm one of the chosen ones. I'm just tryin' to clean up the mess you got into tonight."

Nathan looked at him, unmoved.

"Remember, we could've left you in there to deal with your crazy girlfriend. How'd you end up tied up anyway? You and the sister were gettin' busy when your girl showed up, right?"

"Naw, man. The crazy bitch snuck up from behind me and knocked me cold. When I woke up, she had control."

Frank shook his head.

"I always heard hell hath no fury like a woman scorned."

"You heard right. And if you're dealing with a black woman, then it's really a bitch. But she's got it all wrong, we weren't . . . "

Frank waved his hand, interrupting Nathan's explanation.

"Personally, I don't care if you was bangin' both of them together, one at a time, or at Hart Plaza in broad daylight. All I'm interested in is what's in the Bible."

Nathan acknowledged Frank with a nod before walking over to his entertainment system that held everything, from a 37-inch color TV, DVD/ VCR, to his impressive CD and album collection. He glanced at Frank before opening a drawer on the console.

He froze when he came across the loaded .38-caliber snub-nosed revolver. Thinking briefly about making a play for it, his thoughts of retaliation were interrupted by the monotone voice behind him.

"Be careful now," Frank advised. "We're not pals yet."

Nathan's hand moved aside and grabbed the Bible instead. He turned and faced Frank, who smiled when he saw the religious book in his hand.

"Now we're gettin' somewhere."

He gestured to the couch.

"Well, bro, don't keep me in suspense. Come show me what you got."

Nathan looked at the portly man sitting on his couch, wondering if he should make a move. He could take his fat ass. "Your intentions would be a lot clearer if you didn't have that gun on me," Nathan countered.

"Don't worry about it."

Then the portly restaurant owner did something Nathan was not expecting.

He put the gun on the coffee table, within easy reach if Nathan chose to make a play for it.

The young hustler looked at the gun on the table before he took a seat next to this odd man.

"Here," he said, handing the Bible to Frank. "See for yourself."

Frank Collazo wasn't a religious man, but he knew what the Bible meant to different people. Old man Jenkins saw it as an important part of his life, something he held close to his heart. Nathan Littlejohn, raised in the church as a child, viewed it as the one constant in an otherwise turbulent upbringing. He would lean heavily on its teachings as he grieved for his brother. Frank Collazo, hoping it had the information he was seeking, only saw it as the answer to a puzzling question.

He looked at Nathan's Bible. Sure enough, it was an exact duplicate of the old man's. He flipped through the thick religious book with the gold lettering, and stopped when he got to the Gospel according to Saint John. In one aspect, the Bible was different than the one he had.

Many of the passages were underlined.

The passages in red.

The words of Jesus Christ.

"The old man told me you know your Bible," the older Italian man said to the young African-American.

"Well, I'm no Sunday school teacher, but . . . "

"You could explain this to me then," Frank said, cutting him off. He pointed to the underlined passage.

Nathan read silently for a moment, before he repeated the sentences aloud.

"'I have not a devil; but I honor my Father, and ye do dishonour me.'"

Nathan glanced up at the restaurant owner. His face told him to continue.

"'If I honour myself, my honour means nothing: it is my Father that Honourth me . . . '"

"Stop!" Frank interrupted. "I've heard enough."

He sat silently, staring out into the apartment, not seeing the walls where the impressive artwork of Carl Owens hung, not hearing the calls of the two women in the other room for Nathan Littlejohn. His mind was on his father, who he hadn't thought about in years, till this whole thing started. He couldn't even remember the last time he . . .

Suddenly, it came to him. The answer he was looking for was staring at him, underlined in that Bible.

"This is old man Jenkins' Bible, isn't it?"

He looked up for an answer, only to see the gun now in Nathan Littlejohn's hand.

"Yup," the young man smiled. "I got copies of those letters too."

Frank shook his head.

"You don't understand. I know why old man Jenkins put me in touch with you. The answers' in that Bible."

Nathan was getting impatient. He's been on the run for the last 24 hours, with little or no sleep, his plan for getting rich was falling apart around him, his lady thought that he was fuckin' her sister and planned to do a extreme Lorena Bobbit on him, and he knew his boy, Jenkins, was certainly dead. But the worse part, the part that had him sick to his stomach, was the fact that he was responsible for his brother's murder. He wasn't in the mood for guessing games. After slipping on a T-shirt and a velour Versace jogging suit from his front closet, Nathan was ready for some answers.

"My boy, Jenks. He's dead, isn't he?"

Frank nodded.

He pointed the gun at Frank's head.

"If you don't start makin' sense, you'll be joining him soon."

Enough incentive for Frank.

"This much I know," the short man began. "The man who killed your brother and the man who killed my father is one and the same. Same one you got that serious cash withdrawal from."

"Johnny Salvatore."

"The one and only."

Nathan thought about it for a moment and began to understand how "Greektown Johnny" was on to them so fast. He couldn't ignore the Jenkins connection. When Jenks was on the hunt for cocaine, it didn't matter where his urges led him.

Even to a place they were going to hit less than twenty-four hours later.

"Jenks was spotted at one of the dope houses, wasn't he?"

"That's how I figured. John knew who he was and thought he could beat the info out of him. I saw the tape. Not pretty."

Nathan pointed the gun at the bedroom.

"What about your boy? What's his story?"

"Believe it or not, Johnny killed his father too."

Nathan shook his head.

"So he's hot for 'Greektown Johnny' then."

Frank nodded in agreement and hoped the young man believed what he was told.

"Your boy out there," Nathan said, motioning to the other room, "I hope he's as smart as you."

He lowered the gun from Frank's chest.

"I'm not sure why, but I think I can trust you. Call 'Mike' and tell him everything's cool and to chill. He can relax on my girls out there."

Frank looked at the barrel of his gun aimed at his chest.

"You'd be more convincing if you didn't have my gun in my face."

Nathan looked at him for a minute before he went back over to the entertainment center and pulled the .38 caliber out. He stuck it in his waist before opening Frank's automatic, pulling the clip and emptying its contents before handing it, handle first, to Frank.

"I'll just hold on to these until we become better aquainted," he said as he put the bullets in his pocket. "We might become pals yet."

Frank smiled as he pocketed the .45-caliber automatic.

"Maybe. We got a common enemy, someone who would like to see us both dead. That should mean something."

"Then your partner can chill on holding my girl and her sister hostage then, right?"

"Apparently."

Frank walked over to the closed bedroom door and rapped lightly on the door.

"Yeah?" came the gruff response.

"Cut 'em loose, Mike. I got what we came for."

Slowly, the door of the bedroom opened and the three occupants emerged. The sisters were relieved that their situation was over and that they apparently were going to be permitted to leave. Mike Garbarini looked over at his friend of thirty years and smiled, seeing the Bible in his hand.

Then he felt a burning sensation.

If you listened close, really close, you could hear it.

Barely audible.

Below the murmur of the talking Day sisters was the sound of a dull thud, similar to the sound a mallet makes when it hits a thick side of meat. That's what it sounded like. What it was was the sound a bullet makes when it enters the body. The bullet came from the barrel of a .32-calliber assassin's rifle fired from across the alley. It came through the window that Jeri opened earlier, finding its way through Michael Garbarini's back to his heart. He was dead ten seconds after hitting the ground. A lot of things happened in Mike's last ten seconds. Across town, a man sneaking a midnight snack scratched his lottery ticket, discovering he was $25,000 richer. A woman on the north end decided now was the time to wake her husband and announce she was HIV-positive. Then stab him for giving her the disease.

Michael Garbarini's last ten seconds were like his previous twenty-seven years.

Full of pain and confusion.

But now, his suffering was over.

"GET DOWN!" Nathan yelled as he threw himself at the two women, pulling them down to the hardwood floor.

Frank Collazo looked over at the window for half a second before following Nathan and the Day sisters to the floor. Then it began.

The front window shattered as the sound of an AK-47dominated the early morning. The apartment was being taken apart by flying lead. The Carl Owens paintings, along with the 37-inch color TV/DVD/

VCR player, most of the entertainment center, and the expensive LP collection that was on display next to his Bose stereo system, was destroyed. When the deadly projectiles hit the 155-gallon aquarium, it shattered, sending pieces of thick glass flying through the room, flooding the apartment with water and oxygen-deprived fish. One piece found it's way into Jeri Day's left calf, who announced its arrival with a painful scream.

Then, as suddenly as it began, it stopped, just as the occupants of apartment 520 were beginning to show signs of life.

"You guys okay?" Nathan asked between coughs.

The two women were coughing up dust and smoke as they acknowledged Nathan. Frank Collazo said nothing as he crawled over the debris to where his childhood friend lay, his eyes staring out in an unblinking gaze, similar to the eyes of the piranha that now lay throughout the room, gasping for life. He turned and looked at the survivors.

"We got to get out of here now! They'll be coming up to check their scores."

Nathan looked at the cut Jeri received. Not too bad.

After wrapping a piece of cloth around the wound with one of the torn sheets that earlier held him captive, he was satisfied it would be okay. Then he made his move towards the destroyed entertainment center. Lying on the floor, beside his broken marijuana tray and his LP of Miles Davis' greatest hits, was another gun, this one a loaded 22. He grabbed it and crawled back over towards the women. Now he was ready.

The four targets left the destroyed apartment, only to be detained in the hallway by most of the tenants of the fifth floor. Mrs. Whitmore, with her five cats, was first on the scene. She lived across the hall and often complained about the noise coming from his apartment. Guess he couldn't blame her this time. She was followed by Mr. Gene Littles, the resident know-it-all who was constantly giving advice to Nathan about women, even though at age 44, he still lived with his mother. The dark hallway soon filled with the residents from the other floors, some of whom were convinced that a bomb had gone off, where others felt the police had again raided the wrong building, like they did last summer. Then a face appeared out of the crowd whom Nathan Littlejohn did not want to see. It belonged to the building super, Carlton Simpson.

"What in tarnation is going on here?"

Nathan wondered what tarnation was.

"Boy, what you done now?" he demanded as he pushed his way through the crowd.

"I don't know what happened, Mr. Simpson," he lied. "Must have been a gas leak or something."

Simpson sniffed the air.

"I don't smell no gas."

The widower looked into the destroyed apartment, his mouth dropping open.

Bullet holes decorated the walls. Water from the destroyed aquarium flowed into the hall as the crowd gathering outside the war zone tried to squeeze in the small doorway to get a better view.

"Shit," the agitated super groaned. "Who's that white man layin' on the floor? Who's gonna clean up this mess? What the fuck did you do, Nathan?"

He turned to see Nathan Littlejohn heading down the stairs, past the new tenant who stayed on the corner apartment.

"NATHAN!"

They could hear the super's angry voice calling his name as the four people made their way down the stairs.

"Guess your rent just went up," Frank commented as he led the way to the first floor.

"I was thinkin' about movin', anyway," Nathan countered quickly.

"Forget the jokes, Nathan," Jeri spoke up. "What are we going to do? They were trying to kill us."

"It's not cool being on the receiving end of a gun, is it, sweetheart?" he asked coldly.

She remained silent.

"Come on, you guys, knock it off," the other Day sister piped in. "We've got to get out of here."

"Why don't we trade them laughing boy over there?" Jeri said, gesturing towards Frank.

"In case you didn't notice, they were shooting at me too."

"Maybe they were just after you and we were in the crossfire."

"Maybe you're just an idiot."

Before Jeri could come up with a snappy comeback, Nathan threw his hands up, signaling for quiet.

"If you both don't shut up, you're gonna lead 'em right to us," he said with a raging whisper. "I'm not ready to deal with those bastards yet. We need firepower."

He looked over at Frank.

"I know you connected, man. When we get out, you gonna come through for us, right?"

He pointed his .38 at Frank.

"That's not necessary, Nathan," he said as he peered through the door into the front hallway. "We're pals, remember?"

Nathan grunted.

"I'll take that as a yes. Besides, I've got a plan."

As the four people in the dark stairwell huddled together, the owner of one of the most successful pizza franchises in Metro Detroit explained his idea to them.

After a little discussion, they agreed that it would be safer if the two sisters went out and got the car. They wouldn't attract as much attention. In all the confusion, between the residents and the police and firemen on the scene, they should be able to ease their way out. There was a side exit to the building that was concealed by a huge trash dumpster. It was there they would meet.

Nathan peeked out into the lobby, watching the activity the violence caused the normally quiet building.

Good. No mob types lurking around.

"I don't see anybody who looks suspicious," the perspiring Italian said, reading Nathan's mind. "The time to move is now."

The two women were preparing to leave the men in the dark stairwell when Frank had one last reminder.

"Remember," he said quietly. "Walk quickly without running. Don't draw any attention to yourselves."

He reached into his pocket and gave Tia the keys to the dead man's 88 Buick. He gave Jeri his .45 automatic.

"My car's in front. A dark Buick. All these cops around, it's safe to head out now. Whoever did this is long gone."

"What makes you so sure?" Tia asked as she took the keys.

"No time to check their scores. We didn't run into any shooters on the stairwell. They wouldn't trust the elevator. They would've taken the stairs."

She remained unconvinced.

"We're lucky the twelfth precinct is around the corner. Too many cops for their liking. You satisfied?"

The two sisters looked at Nathan, who hesitated for a minute, then nodded his approval. Jeri opened her mouth to say something, but was interrupted by Nathan's finger across her lips.

"Don't say another word," he said, pulling her close and gently kissing her forehead. "We'll talk later. Oh yeah," he said, reaching in to his pocket.

"You might need these." He opened her hand and dropped the bullets he removed from Frank's gun earlier into it. She looked at him for a second, then her sister.

"You ready, girl?" she asked Tia.

She nodded.

After putting the now loaded gun in a paper bag found on the stairwell, the two women calmly opened the door and strolled out in to the lobby passing through the crowd of panicking residents gathering. There were a couple of cops taking statements, trying without success to produce answers to the many questions being thrown at them.

"What was all that shootin' about? I heard gunshots. Thought I was back in "Nam" for a minute. You cops see a fat white man come through here with anybody? I heard there was a white man upstairs dead." After a couple of heart attack inducing minutes where the cops were overly interested in the good-looking sisters, they made their way out the front door. Now the two men had to make their way around to the side entrance without being seen. They couldn't wait to see if the two women could make it to the car. They had to make it.

"This way," Nathan directed Frank through the dark corridor. "I used to complain to the super 'bout the lights' always bein' broke."

Guiding the restaurateur through the darkness with his butane lighter, the tall black man led them to the side entrance. The heavy metal door creaked open behind their combined weight. It was rarely used, as was evident in the rusted door hinges.

Peeking out of the side entrance door, they could see up the alley to the front, where all the activity was. Police and fire truck lights destroyed the darkness.

It was quite a sight, actually. But the sight the two men were excited to see was the '88 Buick sedan cruising up the alley. No one was following the car, and as it got closer, they could see the beautiful faces of the Day sisters, Tia sitting behind the wheel, trying to stay cool, and Jeri in the back. Both looked worried. The car slowed up and the back door opened, where Jeri sat with her injured leg up on the seat. She had the .45 automatic ready, just in case things didn't go smoothly.

The two men entered the car quickly, Nathan sliding in the back with Jeri and Frank jumping in the front passenger seat.

"You guys get low," Jeri said as the car began moving towards the activity at the front of Nathan Littlejohn's apartment building and on to Woodward Ave.

"I think we're gonna make it, kids," Frank said optimistically. He was looking for any signs of "Greektown Johnny." He saw none.

"Let's go to my place," Frank offered. "There's something there I need to pick up. Head for 696. When you get there, take the westbound until you hit Telegraph North. Take it till you get to Maple, then make a right. I'll give you directions once we get into my subdivision."

"Whoa, dude, slow down," Nathan said. "I haven't decided if I trust you enough for all that." Frank yawned. He needed a few minutes of shut-eye to see him through to the end. It was almost over. He could feel it.

"Look, Nathan," the tired Italian said. "This thing is almost over. You need to trust somebody if you all expect to come out of this alive. Now I've gotten beat up, slapped around, had guns pointed at me, and finally shot at tonight. I'm tired. I'm gonna close my eyes for a minute. If you don't think you can trust me, do what you gotta do." With that, he closed his eyes, letting the drama of the last few hours take a break.

"If I nod off, wake me when we get to Woodland Groves. That's where my place is."

The two people in the back were silent, both lost in deep thought. Jeri now felt she misjudged the situation between Nathan and her sister, but still, she had many questions. Now wasn't the time to ask them. She just wanted to relax. She looked out the window as they entered the ramp leading to I-696.

Suddenly, she remembered Kay Brown sitting in her car, in front of Nathan's apartment. In all the excitement, she forgot about her encounter with Kay. She'd tell Nathan about it when she got a chance. She'd have to get her car from over there before the neighborhood punks stripped it. Jeri didn't have to worry about her car being stripped in Palmer Park.

It wasn't there anymore.

It was on the 696 Freeway, about a half a city block behind them.

Kay Brown was driving the hot-wired Porsche 924. She possessed many talents that she picked up from life on the streets. Hot-wiring cars was one. Learning about men and guns was another. As she drove west on the expressway, she thought about her life at the club and how it has led her to this moment. There were always Mafia types hanging out at the topless club. Most of them were hoping to score with her, but she held most of them in contempt.

Except for one guy. Well, maybe two.

The young mob guy working the club told her he liked her. That he cared for her. That he was in love with her. She saw the way he looked at her when she first started. He always did make nice with her. Kept all those stupid gangsters off her ass while she worked. But they had to lay low. It wouldn't work if his "crew" knew he was keepin' company with a black girl. A dancer, no less. Well, no matter. She occasionally fucked him and spanked him and that was all. It's not like she was his woman, no matter what he thought. She glanced over at her passenger.

That was who she wanted. She wanted to be in a position where she was respected. *Entering a room on this man's arm would do it,* she thought foolishly. She was tired of being looked at as just a sex toy. She controlled men in the bedroom. Working her magic in the outside world proved more difficult.

But this was the man who could make it happen.

Over the last few months, she was doing her best to make herself indispensable to him and it seemed to be working, for the most part. Sometimes, he could be a real asshole. She looked at the man next to her, adjusting her position in her seat so her loose-fitting top was slightly open. She knew he got a cheap thrill peeking at her well-formed breasts.

"Why so quiet?"

She hesitated before answering his question, wary of the response she would get for questioning anything concerning him.

Nervously, "Thinkin' 'bout tonight, baby. Surprised you called for a ride after I seen you at Jimmy's. Why'd you point me out to Nathan? I was just havin' a little fun with him, that's all."

She rubbed her jaw at the spot where the butt end of Jeri Day's 9mm connected. A dark bruise marked the spot. She hoped he would notice and show his concern by asking about it. He didn't.

"Nice Porsche," the gangster asked, ignoring her question. "Where'd you get it?"

"When I got to Jimmy's, I hooked up with a girlfriend," she lied. "You know what? The bitch ended up leaving with some nigga so she asked me to keep it 'til she got back."

"That why it's hot-wired?" he said, pointing out the loose wires hanging from underneath the dashboard. "She didn't have time to toss you her keys?"

She glanced into his eyes for a second before returning them to the freeway, where she saw the Buick they were following exit onto Telegraph. He chuckled slightly, making a mental note about her lying to him.

"I told you to get him out tonight, not play games with him. Remember, you only see him 'cause I allow it." Their verbal sparring went one more round.

"I know you didn't mean it," she purred. "But when you said you only keep me around because of my looks, that hurt."

He looked at her, surprised.

"And I earn the money I make. It ain't easy gettin' up there dancin' every night."

"I know, baby," he said, smiling. "I hate those fuckers leerin' at you all night."

He reached over and put his hand on her thigh, rubbing it.

"But let's face it. You're the hottest dancer I got. You bring in the money. You're the one they come to see, so we gotta deal with it."

She looked over at the man the papers called "Detroit's Most Dangerous Criminal," disappointment all over her face.

"You not ready to quit on me, are ya?"

"You know I'm not, baby."

"Good," he said, smiling. "Nobody quits on me. Some have tried, but they ain't around no more." He squeezed her thigh. "Know what I mean?"

Sparring over. Victory: "Greektown Johnny."

Maybe John Salvatore wasn't ready to settle down yet, but she hoped that, with time, she just might hit the jackpot.

CHAPTER EIGHTEEN

The '88 Buick that was northbound on Telegraph Road was doing the allowable speed of 50 mph. The last thing the four people in the car needed was to get stopped for some stupid violation and have to explain why they were driving through one of southeast Michigan's richest communities with a loaded .45-caliber automatic, a .38-caliber snub-nosed revolver, a .22 "midnight special" and a Walther PPK semiautomatic that also discharged .38-caliber slugs. Fortunately, they made it to the pizza king's house with no incident.

The two sisters were impressed by the two-and three-story houses, with the perfectly manicured lawns that dominated the subdivision. The new trees that lined the circular streets told them this place was only a couple of years old, not decades old, like the projects the sisters grew up in. Their wide eyes spoke volumes. This did not go unnoticed by Frank Collazo.

"There's my place on the corner," Frank pointed. "Pull into the driveway."

Frank Collazo's three-story, six-bedroom colonial rested on a half acre that sat on top of a hill, at the end of Woodland Groves. The massive house covered over 5,000 square feet. It had cathedral ceilings, a fully stocked cellar that held some of the world's rarest wines, a huge game room filled with the latest video games, a professional sized pool table, and one of those 60-inch plasma TV's hanging on the wall that Nathan dreamed of buying with his new fortune. The pizza king also had a shooting gallery, where he practiced the manly art of discharging rare and often illegal firearms. This is what working nonstop all these years meant to him.

After reading the underlined passages in the Bible, he realized that he needed to change what had been motivating his existence. And he felt it would begin tonight.

After they entered his house through the four-car garage, they made their way through the spectacular kitchen to the spacious family room, where he instructed them to have a seat.

"I've got a few things to take care of," he said as he motioned to the basement. "Just in case we have visitors."

"Go ahead, man," Nathan said, looking out the huge glass door panel that held a spectacular view of the immaculate backyard. "We got it covered up here."

When their host headed down the stairs, Nathan walked across the room, where he made himself quite comfortable behind the bar. Once there, he began looking at the row of exotic liquors that lined the back shelf, like a professional bartender preparing to make a cocktail. When he came across a bottle of Jack Daniels, he stopped. Before he reached the Kentucky Bourbon, he was interrupted by Jeri's hand on his arm.

"This is incredible, ain't it?"

"Yep," he said, turning to face her. "This is what I'm talkin' about. This is how I want my shit to lay," he said, looking around the impressive room. "Smooth and elegant." He took her hand. "Come here for a minute," he said, leading her across the room to the huge door panel facing the backyard.

Then he turned and drew her close to him.

"Look, baby," he began. "I don't know where you got it in your head that me and Tia were . . . "

Jeri put her finger up to his lips, preventing him from continuing.

"Sshhh. I don't wanna talk about it anymore. I just want to tell you how sorry I am for hittin' you and trippin' the way I did. It's just that when I seen you guys outside your apartment, you was lookin' all cozy."

"What you talkin' about?"

"I don't know," she said, walking around the large room. "I could hear ya'll talkin' and I heard Tia say you shouldn't be with her in the first place and after what I saw and what Kay Brown told me, I thought you meant me."

Hearing that Jeri talked to Kay Brown that evening made Nathan's mind go into overdrive.

"When did you talk to her? What did she tell you?"

At the sound of Kay's name, Tia came from exploring the kitchen back into the family room.

"We hooked up at Belle Isle."

"Belle Isle?" they both said in unison.

"Yeah. I followed her. When you and Tia drove off, I figured I'd set Miss Thang straight on a few things."

"You were at Jimmy's. So what happened?"

"We got physical for a sec until I brought the noise out. She said ya'll been bonin', which I figured. But when she said you and Tia had been together, my mind snapped."

After everything they'd been through tonight, Nathan knew his days of lying to this woman was over.

"You're lucky she didn't pop you with my nine. The bitch lifted it from my car sometime tonight." Nathan looked deeply into Jeri's eyes, hoping to convince her of his sincerity.

"I won't lie. Me and Kay been hangin' a little, but nothin' ever happened between Tia and me. I just needed to find out what Kay knew about the job we did yesterday."

Jeri didn't say a word. She just looked at him, then at her sister.

"I swear, we ain't never done nothin'. Only reason I was with Kay tonight was to break it off. I told her it was over and if you seen us on Woodward, you know I'm tellin' the truth."

"He's right. He was tryin' to cut me loose."

They all turned around, startled to see Kay Brown standing at the door to the garage. She was holding a .25-caliber on them.

"I don't know what he's talkin' about as far as his gun goes. I got my own right here." She showed off the gun, like a woman showing off her diamond engagement ring.

"Don't be so hard on him, Jeri," she began as she walked towards them, keeping the gun high. "He thinks he's in love with you. What the hell, it don't matter to me. We had our fun using each other. But that's over. It's time to get real."

She looked around, glancing into the kitchen and then out the door wall, where she could see the backyard. She hit a switch on the wall, illuminating the backyard.

"All right, guys, where's our host?"

"Fuck you," Jeri responded.

Kay Brown looked at her and smiled. Pointing the gun at her chest, she walked over and smacked her across the face.

"Didn't you have enough at the park?"

Jeri rubbed her face, glaring at Kay Brown.

"We gonna get busy again. Count on it."

"Yeah, whatever," Kay replied. "I'm gonna ask you again."

She pressed the gun against Jeri's head.

"Where is Frank Collazo? Nathan?"

Kay's ex-lover shrugged his shoulders.

"I don't know. It's a big house."

Suddenly, the door to the garage opened and a man stepped through. A large, heavyset man of Italian descent, he walked in and instantly took charge with his presence alone.

"After all these years," he said, looking around. "You know this is my first time at Frank's house."

Nathan did a double-take. Just like in the movies. That voice. The man on the street outside of Jimmy's.

"'Greektown Johnny' Salvatore."

The godfather smiled.

"Well, well," he said, walking over to stand directly in front of Nathan. "Nathan Littlejohn, the one most responsible for rippin' me off. Did you really think you could touch me for close to half a mill and get away clean?"

"Was it that much, John? I really didn't have time to count it."

He flashed a big smile back at the gangster.

"I know. I hear you been busy. I've been busy myself tryin' to catch up to you."

Without warning, Nathan's stomach tried to make instant contact with Nathan's spine, courtesy of John's right fist.

"Caught up to your brother though, didn't I?" the mobster said, flashing his killer smile.

Nathan didn't respond. He was doubled over on his knees, trying to get the air back in his lungs.

"It's not the amount of money you stole that pisses me off. You made me look weak. I can't let you get away with that."

"Now I gotta admit one thing," Johnny continued as he turned and walked back into the garage. When he reappeared, he was carrying a Louisville Slugger baseball bat.

"You showed some balls, the way you took care of my boys. I'm gonna have a hard time replacing 'em."

Nathan's eyes grew wide as he remembered the scene from *The Untouchables*. You know, the one where Robert de Niro did a hellava Al Capone with a beat down that made Hollywood history. He started sweating. Where the hell was Frank Collazo?

"Hey, Frank!" the mobster yelled out.

What, could he read minds too?

"Frank, come on out. I'm about to do some redecoratin' in here. You think blood-red is gonna clash with this pretty white carpet? Frank? FRANK!"

Unknown to the occupants of the house, Frank Collazo had a perfect view of the family room. He had worked his way up the back stairs and was watching the action below from a hall closet. He knew he had to make a move fast if he wanted to save the people downstairs.

"Oh, God, no. Help us, please help us," Tia day began repeating over and over.

Kay Brown walked over to where the young woman stood.

"Shut up, bitch," she said as she gave Tia a hard backhand, quieting her instantly.

Nathan glanced over at the wet bar in the corner, where their weapons sat on top, cursing himself for letting his guard down for that brief moment.

Then he focused.

There were only two guns on the top of the bar. The PPK and the .38 snub-nose. He looked over at Jeri, who smiled at him. He then knew she was still packing.

As Kay dealt with Tia, Frank knew his time had come. He couldn't wait for Johnny to decide to stop playing around and pull his gun. He had to make his move. He poked his assassin's rifle with the infrared scope out from the cracked hall-closet door and took aim. He decided long before that he didn't want to kill Johnny. Not yet. He needed to hear him admit that he killed his father and set up Mike. He hoped Nathan was quick. He wouldn't have much time before Johnny would pull his own gun and begin blasting. He took aim through the scope.

"Well, Nathan," the godfather began, "I guess Frank ain't gonna come out and play with us. I'll deal with him later. He's hidin' out like the chicken shit I knew he was."

He walked over to Nathan again, slapping the fat end of the bat in his hand.

"Before I start playin' ball with your head, boy, you're gonna tell me where my money is. If you think I'm bullshittin', remember your apartment. And your brother."

Nathan's light brown eyes grew dark.

"I should have brought my boys with me from your place," Johnny said, looking at the Day sisters.

"They would've had fun with your girls while we're busy gettin' to know each other. But this arrangement is good. This way, your bitches can see how stupid you've been." The gangster started swinging the bat as if he was in the batter's box at Yankee Stadium, waiting for his chance against Roger Clemens.

"A word of advice. Always keep your business separate from the bedroom. You never know who else your bitch is fuckin'."

Nathan glared at Kay Brown, who returned his icy stare with a smirk.

Suddenly, Nathan noticed a red dot appear on Kay's arm. Unnoticed by the gangster and his accomplice, the dot moved down her arm and settled on the wrist of her gun hand.

"I got one question," Nathan said, anticipating the drama of the next few minutes. "How do you feel about kissing the mouth that's been sucking this dick?"

The gangster's gray eyes turned dark with anger.

"Okay, smart boy," Johnny sneered. "Batter up."

The next few seconds changed everything.

There was a muffled pop. Then a scream.

The .38 slug from Frank's assassin's rifle shattered Kay's right hand, hitting it at the wrist. Blood shot from the wound like a ruptured water hose, spraying the carpet red. It had the effect of an out of control graffiti artist who lost control of his paint can. As Kay Brown stood there, screaming and holding what was left of her hand, Johnny turned his head. That was all the time Nathan needed. At that point, Nathan tackled the mob boss at his knees, just like they taught him in Little League football many years before. He could hear the crack of the mobster's left knee, signaling an injured anterior cruciate ligament or other such injury. He let out a horrific scream, dropping the bat as he was driven to the floor. Jeri pulled her gun and pointed it at "Greektown Johnny" as he writhed on the floor in pain while Tia's fist exploded repeatedly in to Kay's face, knocking her unconscious and quieting her screams.

"Shut up, BITCH!" she said with emphasis. She looked over at her sister and Nathan, smiling.

"Good job, man," Nathan congratulated as Frank came down the stairs.

"Yeah, but my carpet is ruined. You know how much it's gonna cost me to replace it?"

Nathan laughed.

"I got a couple thou I could loan you, if you good for it."

The four people laughed nervously, sensing that the nightmare of the past day was over.

"Shit. Get me an ambulance," the crime boss moaned as he clutched his swelling knee. "FUCK."

"Not so fast, Johnny," Frank said as he leaned over the fallen godfather.

He reached into the gangster's sports coat and removed the .45 he always carried.

"Now, I want you to tell me what happened the nights my dad and Mike's dad got killed."

"Fuck you, Collazo," he responded. "I wouldn't tell you shit."

They picked the mobster off the floor and put him on the couch.

"You girls get something to wrap that chick's wrist up before she bleeds to death. Take her to the bathroom, down the hall to the left," the pizza man instructed.

They complied.

"Now," the angry young man demanded as he leaned on the injured man's knee. "TALK!"

After a few well-placed kicks, the most powerful criminal in Detroit couldn't deal with the pain, so he began singing like Sinatra. He was with Mike when his father busted them while they were smoking in the alley. He followed them back to their place and when he listened at the door of their apartment, he could hear Mike getting beaten. Before he knew what was happening, he busted down the door and attacked old man Garbarini. In his rush to assist his partner against his out of control father, he forgot an important part of this violent melodrama. Although he was decently put together for his age, he had not yet begun his legendary workouts, perfecting the impressive physic he now displays. This was the catalyst for those hundreds of hours spent with exercise equipment over the years. Old man Garbarini man-handled him. Worked him over good. He blacked out and when he came to, Mike was gone, Little Tony was there with the gun and old man Garbarini was lying on the floor unconscious.

"So you was there when Mike was gettin' beat down," Frank stated. "Mike didn't tell me that. I guess he called himself protectin' you. So then what?"

The gangster continued with his sorry story of deceit and betrayal. Mike didn't know Tony came by the apartment with the gun. He's the one who got Johnny up and out. But not before Johnny settled things with Mr. Garbarini as he laid on the floor.

"You know what?" the gangster admitted, confirming their suspecions about his sanity, "It felt good, takin' that scum out."

"But you didn't want to take the credit," Nathan piped in.

"You mean the blame," Frank corrected. "So you and Tony was in on it. That's what he was blackmailin' you with."

"Oh, so you know about that, huh? I knew you were smart, Collazo."

The crime lord continued the story, explaining how he convinced Tony not to tell the police what really happened. He told him that old man Garbarini deserved what he got and Mike wouldn't be held because he only hit him with a hammer. The cops knew he wasn't bludgeoned to death. When Mike went to the cops, it was easy for them to force a confession out of him, no problem to convict him.

"So you and Tony just let him rot in jail. I knew you were sick, not having any feelings for anybody but yourself, but Tony? I can't believe he went along with it," Frank grumbled.

"He had no choice. Not if he didn't want to take Mike's place. He was an accessory to murder. He would've gotten twenty years. And I wasn't doin' no time."

"How was Tony an accessory?" Frank wondered. "You pulled the trigger."

"I needed assurances that Tony wouldn't rat me out to the cops or anybody else. So I convinced him to take a shot at the old bastard."

"No way Tony shot Mike's dad," Frank replied. "He was one of us, not a psycho like you."

"After what he just saw he wasn't tryin to argue with me. Plus I helped him squeeze the trigger. It wasn't too hard convincing old Tone that he was in deep shit too."

"You're a wicked muthafucka," Nathan commented.

"That's when Tony disappeared," Frank added. "You knew if he stayed, he would've come clean."

"I knew he wouldn't keep quiet so I convinced him to leave town."

"I'm surprised you didn't just kill him too."

The criminal looked Frank Collazo in the eye. "What, you think I'm a monster? He was my friend."

The two men looked at each other with disbelief, before the gangster continued.

"Like I told ya. Takin' out that shit Garbarini felt good to me. It was like I finally found my calling. Garbarini was in deep shit with the mob over some gambling debts. They was nervous about him cryin to the boys in blue so I did em' a favor takin his ass out. Somehow, the crew found out about him getting it and they wanted to find the guy who did it. I figured it was my chance to hit the big time so I let them know I was their boy."

The crime boss glowed as he reflected on his murderous beginnings.

"The next thing I knew, I was gettin' contracts. Kill this bum, take that guy out, ya know. And I was good at it. I only made one mistake."

"And what was that?"

"My boss wanted me to talk to your old man. He knew you and me hung out and he figured your old man might listen to me. He was already cleanin' money for us, but that wasn't enough. He wanted to be in, like he was a made man, but it wasn't layin' like that."

The mobster hesitated until Nathan put additional pressure on his knee. His loud groan told them he would continue.

"He was always bustin' our balls about what he knew. Pretty soon, it wasn't safe for him to be anywhere but around us. We needed to keep an eye on him to see exactly how big a mouth he had. The boys started makin' noise about how much trouble he could make. He didn't know it but the only thing keepin' him alive was his friendship with the Don."

"What friendship? My father never hung out with any gangsters."

The fallen mob boss laughed, then groaned.

"You don't know what the fuck your old man was into. He hung out at the gambling spots and the whorehouses like everybody else. All you saw was the hard-working family man. I saw him layin' up at Ms. Ada's house on Second, gettin' some pussy. Did you know that your father liked black whores?"

In the blink of an eye, Frank Collazo's fist exploded into the face of John Salvatore.

"YOU'RE A GODDAMN LIAR!"

The godfather's nose broke with the blow, sending blood flowing out onto his shirt and the floor.

"Damn, Frank," Nathan said taking a step back from the bleeding man.

"I didn't know you had it in ya," Johnny chuckled, holding his nose. Then he laughed again before continuing.

"I was there collectin' one night when I seen him upstairs. I followed him up to a room, gave him a couple minutes to get busy, and then I peeked in. Your old man was tied to the bed and the whore was on top. When he seen me lookin', I thought he was gonna shit on himself."

The hustler and the pizza man looked at each other, thinking the same thing.

Women tying men to beds have been around for a while.

"Anyway, I went to see him that night, at the store. I told him what his options were, but he wasn't havin' it. He thought because he saved Don Borsellino's life once, the rules no longer applied to him. It was my job to make him understand that wasn't the case."

"Who was Don Borsellino?" Nathan asked.

"He was John's boss," Frank answered. "His first boss. The man who hired him."

"And my father saved his life?" he said, turning his attention back to the fallen don. "How?"

"Two men came into his store, askin' about when Don Borsellino would be in. He loved your old man's corned beef. Ate lunch there three times a week. Your old man called and told "the Don" the corned beef was bad that day. He suggested he send somebody to check it out for him. He sent Paul Guido and Giovanni Andreotti."

"Who were they?" asked Nathan.

"Two of the most vicious and successful soldiers they had in their gang," Frank answered. "If I had boys like them today, you wouldn't have come close to touchin' me," the criminal bragged.

"So anyway . . . " Frank prompted.

"So anyway, those two hoods come back looking for "the Don," except they meet Guido and Andreotti."

"What happened?"

"I seen Andreotti after that. He told me the crosstown boys were part of I-94. Anyway, my boss was grateful. That's why he wasn't to be killed."

"But you killed him anyway."

The godfather shrugged.

"Sure, I killed him. I had to. For the good of the family. I knew Don Borsellino would never give the order unless he had no choice. They were friends. That's what clouded his judgment. He couldn't see that his friend was a threat to everything we had goin. The crew was getting restless. Nobody liked your old man with his phony gangster wannabe act. He had a big mouth like you and when I started hearin shit on the streets that had no business out there, I knew where the leak was. You know what happens if you ignore a leakin' pipe? The damage is incredible. The leakin' water fucks up everything. I wasn't gonna ignore our leak. So I fixed it. For good. I gave him my trademark so the boys would know who'd done it."

Frank answered Nathan's question before he could ask it.

"Three in the back, two in the head."

At that moment, Frank knew he could kill Johnny Salvatore with his bare hands. But he didn't. He wanted to see him suffer in jail, like Mike had to do for all those years.

"The truth is finally out," Frank said relieved. "You're going to rot in jail, Johnny. I wish Mike were here to see this, to know you're the one who sold him out."

Nathan walked over to the phone. "You know," he said, pressing the keypad. "There's always something I wanted to do but was never in a position to do till now."

"Operator," he said into the mouthpiece. "Get me the police."

He looked over at the two men smiling. As Nathan gave West Bloomfield's finest the directions to Frank's house, the mob boss glared at him, still clutching his knee in agony.

"I always wanted to say that."

"I'll never do a day in prison," the crime lord boasted. "You got no evidence. I won't even get a ticket for the mess I made at your apartment," he said to Nathan smugly.

"You didn't tell him about the Bible, Frank?" Nathan asked the pizza man.

"I was just about to."

He turned his attention back to the injured gangster.

"You know I couldn't figure out half of this shit if it weren't for Samuel Jenkins Sr. He pointed me in the right direction. I had been working all these years, building up my dad's business, trying to ease my guilt over his death. I drank heavy for years, blamin' myself for what happened."

His eyes became cloudy.

"But Mr. Jenkins helped me understand. He told me that I should honor my father. I thought I was doing that by building up the business. After I come from my yard, you'll know what I'm talkin' about, if you can understand what honor means."

He turned to look at Nathan. "Watch him close."

"Like a hawk" the urban soldier replied.

Frank went out to his backyard, over to a section he had fenced off from the rest of the yard. After a few minutes, he returned, carrying a black shoebox. It was blackened with dirt.

"This box was buried in the back part of my yard. I didn't even know Mr. Jenkins knew where I lived. But he was a smart son of a gun."

He laid the dirty box on the coffee table in the family room and brushed the dirt off from it.

"Did you know my father is buried out there, Johnny?" he asked the mob boss. "Old man Jenkins knew."

With that, Frank opened the box and carefully pulled out an old .45-caliber handgun. A look of recognition came over the mobster's face.

"You wanna bet the slugs from Mike's dad and my father both came from this gun?"

The gangster stared into Frank's eyes, his hatred raging.

"I didn't think so. When you have as many guns lying around your house as you do, it wouldn't be a problem for a disgruntled employee, like a butler, to pull a switch while cleaning his employer's gun cabinet. What do you think, Nathan?"

"Wouldn't be a problem," he sang in support.

"Oh, and one more thing," the pizza man said as he stepped over the fallen mob boss. He crossed the room to the wet bar. Stepping behind the bar, he went right for the bottle of Jack Daniels. Sliding the bottle over, a tiny red dot could be seen. It looked like the little red dot that was on Kay's hand, right before it exploded. It wasn't from an assassin's rifle or any kind of laser pointer. It was the red light of a video camera, signaling a recording in progress. He reached down behind a loose panel and pulled out a small 8-mm tape. Frank Collazo turned and looked at "Greektown Johnny," smiling.

"About that no evidence thing. I don't have to tell you what this is. It's a videotape. A machine called a camcorder records things and a machine called a VCR plays them. Guess what's on this one?"

Before the godfather could answer, the sound of police sirens in the distance began to fill the air.

"Mr. Jenkins took pride in his work. He once told me that his work was never done until he got all the garbage out."

Nathan looked at the fallen crime boss and smiled.

"I guess his work is all done now."

CHAPTER NINETEEN

After the police took "Greektown Johnny" Salvatore, and the ambulance left with Kay Brown, the two new friends took a walk out to the private cemetery, leaving the Day sisters inside to patch up their differences.

There were two headstones in the small graveyard. Frank's mother and father were buried next to each other, side by side, like he promised. Next to his father's grave marker was a section of loose dirt, where the shoebox was buried.

"Let me ask you something, Frank," Nathan began. "How did you know after all this time, that the murder weapon from thirty years ago would be here right under your nose?"

"It's strange, but after looking at those underlined passages in the Bible, it clicked. What Mr. Jenkins told me, how I was honoring material things instead of my father's memory. I just knew the proof I needed would be here. Almost like my father was working with Mr. Jenkins to guide me there."

"Um-hmm. Let me ask you something else. What pissed you off when you broke old boy's nose?" he said, motioning towards the house. The restaurateur looked at Nathan but was interrupted by a yell from the house. The Day sisters stood in the massive doorway.

"COME ON IN, GUYS!" Jeri yelled.

"WE'RE MAKING BREAKFAST," added Tia. "HOW DO YOU LIKE YOUR EGGS, FRANK?"

"Didn't bother you that your daddy was with a black woman, did it?"

Frank looked at Nathan and smiled.

"OVER EASY," he replied, grinning at his new friend. "I LIKE 'EM RUNNY."

"JUST LIKE A WHITE GUY," Tia laughed as she disappeared into the house behind her sister.

"Are you asking me if I got a problem hanging out with beautiful women who just happen to be black?"

He put his hand on Nathan's shoulder.

"Not in this lifetime."

Nathan smiled before turning to admire the sunrise. It was the first time in years he was awake to see it.

It was very calming.

It was going to be a beautiful morning.

*   *   *

That's what the large man on the hill overlooking Frank Collazo's spacious backyard was thinking. What a beautiful morning it was going to be. On his way racing across the city, he listened to the weather guy on the radio confirm it. High around eighty. No humidity. He listened to the birds waking up, filling the air with their music.

How calm everything seemed. Soothing. He didn't think it would be this way. He thought the excitement and the adrenaline would be overwhelming.

He thought he'd be anxious, nervous, maybe a little nauseous.

He heard some of the guys talking once. How some of 'em got sick.

Not him.

He wasn't gonna be a pussy and get sick. He'd show 'em.

He'd show 'em all.

He'd prove to his crew that he could handle things. Important things.

He wasn't just some dope who was only good for fixin' drinks, takin' out the drunks, or runnin' errands. He was more than that. He had ambition. He had goals. He wanted to move up the ladder, just like the lowly mailroom boy at any corporation. So he did what any good worker bee did. He kept his nose to the grindstone. He kept his eyes and ears open. And he kept his mouth shut. He didn't let anybody know what he was doing.

Except his girlfriend.

Well, she wasn't really his girlfriend. What they had, labels couldn't cover. They had something. Maybe it was just mutual need. He wasn't sure. He knew his crew wouldn't understand. Hell, he barely knew what was going on himself. She just seemed to need him, like no one needed him before. It didn't matter that she was black. Not much.

She was good to him. She always made time to speak. Never too busy. That's what he noticed first.

Wrong. That's the second thing he noticed. The first was how tall and sexy she was. That she made time for him, that was cool. Since that first night at Pussycats, she always made time for him.

The basement at the club.

That's where they had their first connection. That's where she discovered him one night after closing, doing his thing. He went to the basement every night after closing. That's where he practiced. Every night.

Every night after he cleaned up all the piss, the nut-jobs from the jackoffs, and the blood, he'd go practice. And you know what?

He was gettin' good. Not as good as Marcello yet, but good.

But would that be good enough? Self-doubt began to creep into his mind. Was he ready? Could he pull this off?

"Come on, baby, now's the time. Johnny's gonna be put down hard if you don't come through. There's nobody else to turn to. You heard what I said. Marcello and Vito are both dead. There's nobody else around. I called the club. *There's nobody else goddamnit!* YOU gotta handle this."

That's what she told him. Convinced him, really.

"You sure you got the directions . . . WHAT? I'M GETTIN' OFF THE PHONE. HOW LONG'S IT GONNA TAKE TO GET TO A

GODDAMN HOSPITAL AND GET MY GODDAMN HAND FIXED?" She turned her attention back to her cell phone. "Damn, this hurts like hell. CAN'T YOU GUYS GIVE ME SOMETHIN' FOR THIS FUCKIN' PAIN? DAMN!" Back to the cell: "I gotta go, baby. We gonna be at the hospital soon . . . I don't know yet . . . yeah, the cops are trailin' the ambulance. When I know what's happenin', I'll call, if I can . . . They said I'm going straight to surgery . . . Yeah, I'm gonna be fine . . . you just remember what you gotta do. Just like we been practicin'. Get those motherfuckas, baby. Stay relaxed, stay focused. You can do this . . . Yeah, I know . . . WE HERE YET? THANK GOD!" Back to the cell: "Yeah baby, we here . . . I don't know . . . WHAT HOSPITAL IS THIS? . . . St. John's on Woodward . . . okay . . . I'll call you . . . good luck."

He could barely make out what she told him. The siren drowned out most of their conversation.

But he got it.

So here he was, at daybreak, lying on his stomach in the woods, on the hill behind the backyard of Frank Collazo, waiting for his chance to impress his crew, and his boss. The huge man, known as Gino to the patrons and dancers at Pussycats Strip Club, lifted the assassin's rifle to his shoulder and peered through the scope at the two men standing in the immaculate backyard. Yup, there they were, just like his girlfriend said they'd be. He smiled as he took aim.

Well, she wasn't really his girlfriend.

Printed in the United States
20650LVS00002BA/53